Girls From da Hood 8

Girls From da Hood 8

Treasure Hernandez

and

Natalie Weber

www.urbanbooks.net

Urban Books, LLC
97 N18th Street
Wyandanch, NY 11798

ISBN 13: 978-1-62286-993-0
ISBN 10: 1-62286-993-1

First Mass Market Printing May 2016
First Trade Paperback Printing August 2013
Printed in the United States of America

10 9 8 7 6 5 4 3 2

This is a work of fiction. Any references or similarities to actual events, real people, living, or dead, or to real locales are intended to give the novel a sense of reality. Any similarity in other names, characters, places, and incidents is entirely coincidental.

Distributed by Kensington Publishing Corp.
Submit Orders to:
Customer Service
400 Hahn Road
Westminster, MD 21157-4627
Phone: 1-800-733-3000
Fax: 1-800-659-2436

Bad Education

by

Treasure Hernandez

1

Gabby

I got off the B54 bus that runs from downtown Brooklyn along Myrtle Avenue, the weight of my backpack slowing me down. The crowd had changed dramatically since I got on at Jay Street on the other side of the socioeconomic divide. There were only a handful of white people left and within a few stops the passengers would all be some shade of brown. I walked past a group of older teenagers in saggy pants leaned up against a wall smoking blunts. They shifted all their focus on me, their prey.

"Yo, mama, wanna play school with me?" One of them leered, slapping palms with his friends.

"Let me see what you got under that uniform," a second added.

"What, you go to Hogwarts?" The first one used that corny-ass *Harry Potter* reference to make fun of my burgundy plaid skirt, white blouse, burgundy vest, and knee socks.

"Baby, I can teach you more than them ABC's." Another, shorter one with busted teeth winked, but I shifted my eyes away and pretended not to notice them.

I decided then and there to ignore any and all the elements of this place that bothered me; and, believe me, there were plenty. Maybe I was a snob. I just didn't understand a neighborhood of people that could have or should have been motivated to climb the economic ladder, but instead they were content hanging outside doing nothing but shooting the shit. And this was during the nine-to-five workday. Yeah, this was the polar opposite of the upwardly mobile neighborhood where I had been raised. I knew I was sounding judgmental, like my mother. She had grown up here and made it her life's mission to never return, but unfortunately there were some things that even she couldn't control. Like me winding up living her nightmare.

Within a few blocks each way, gentrification, fancy wine bars, and Starbucks had sprung up and taken hold; but the aura of poverty within the Cumberland housing projects remained unchallenged and unchangeable.

This wasn't the first time I'd stepped off the bus on Myrtle Avenue to get to my Aunt Kim's tenement apartment, but everything about this trip was different. I was no longer a visitor counting down the minutes until I could escape to the safety and sanity of my own neighborhood. The Cumberland housing projects had become my home whether I liked it or not, and I would have to make the best of it for the time being. Aunt Kim was my mother's younger, wilder sister and my only living relative, unless you counted my father, and I certainly didn't especially since I'd never met him. He and my mother had been high school boyfriend and girlfriend. She had run into him on a trip home a couple of years later and one thing led to another and there she was knocked up. She said his life was already too big to include us, whatever that meant. I assumed it meant that he had another girlfriend in college and had rejected her, wanting more. He hadn't stepped up because my mother raised me on her own until four months ago when she got sick. She was diagnosed with ovarian cancer and her health deteriorated quickly. In the two weeks since she died I'd been walking around nearly catatonic. My aunt had allowed me to stay home from school but yesterday she reminded me that my mother would not appreciate me neglecting the good fortune I had in getting a scholarship to St. Agnes, a pricey private school in toney Brooklyn Heights.

I was a senior and I'd been at St. Agnes since seventh grade and was on track to be the second member of my family to attend a four-year college. My advisor thought I'd be an ideal candidate for the Ivies, so before my mother passed I had applied for five of the eight. Instead of being anxious about admissions letters I no longer cared. Going to Harvard was our dream and without her to hold it up it had already begun to wither. The admissions letters had just been mailed out. I just cared less and less every day about my future and what college I attended, or if I even went to college at all.

"Watch where you going, bitch!" hollered an attractive brown-skinned sister about my age wearing a nasty scowl and a fresh weave. Her clique of three girls surrounded her.

"I'm sorry," I sputtered nervously. I'd been so busy in my own world I hadn't even seen them.

"You better be! What the fuck, you some retard Catholic schoolgirl?" She laughed in my face.

"No, it's not a Catholic School it's a prep school," I answered flatly. All I wanted was to get upstairs and throw myself onto my bed and weep. All day I'd been holding back the urge to fall apart, but I knew my mother would expect more from me so I held it together. And now this?

"No, it's not a Catholic school," a light-skinned girl with bad skin and a tank top two sizes too small mocked me. "Bitch, we don't care about you or your bullshit edumacation. What you need to care about is staying out of Mika's way." She shouted the words at me. I nodded in agreement, just wanting to get out of there. I tried to step past them but they formed a barrier and blocked me from moving. Suddenly a couple of them grabbed my backpack and purse and flung them to the ground.

"Maybe next time that'll help you remember to watch where the fuck you going." Mika pushed up in my face before walking away. This was clearly her way of letting me know that she meant real business. Message received.

I bent down and started picking up the contents of my backpack, shoving them inside the bag. By the time I gathered all my things and stood up the group had moved off to the side, watching my humiliation. As I turned toward the building a tall caramel-colored guy with short, curly hair shot out from around the corner and raced straight at me. Before I could stop him he flung a package into my already overloaded arms. A finger rose to his lips as he caught my eye. He was halfway down the block before I had a chance to react. Next thing, a series of police cars raced past me. The police cars cut him off. Cops jumped out and threw him up against the chain-link fence. Mika and her girls glared at me from their bench across the yard. They had seen everything and it seemed to piss them off more, if that was possible. I hurried into the building before anything else could happen.

I still hadn't gotten used to the overpowering stench of urine that greeted me as I entered the stairwell and raced up six flights of stairs before hurrying into the corridor and the safety of my aunt's apartment. I knew she wouldn't be home when I got here. She worked a nine-to-five on Wall Street and then she usually went to her twelve-step meetings. Although lately she'd been skipping meetings to hang out with her new boyfriend.

My hands were shaking as I let myself into the apartment. I tossed my things down on the floor and flung myself across my bed. I didn't know how long I lay there crying when I heard a banging at the door. It could have been any one of my aunt's neighbors. If I refused to answer the door maybe they would get the hint and go away. But after a full five minutes of relentless banging I dragged myself off the bed and went to answer the door.

2

"Yes," I shouted through the closed door. I knew better than to open it without identifying the visitor. This was not the suburbs. It wasn't even Park Slope, the gentrified neighborhood where I had grown up across from Prospect Park.

"It's me. The guy from outside," I heard a deep smooth voice respond.

"Excuse me?"

"I think you have something that belongs to me," he answered in a tone that said he thought it was a joke.

"I don't open doors for strangers."

"Well if you would open the door and let me introduce myself then I wouldn't be a stranger." He laughed but I didn't bother to respond. All I wanted was to crawl up into a ball, close my eyes, and pretend that my mother was still here.

"How did you find me?"

"I'm not sure you know this but you're the only girl in these parts with a St. Agnes uniform. This neighborhood ain't filled with private school girls so you stick out like a purple giraffe. Some people make it their business to know everything that goes on around here and I make it my business to know those people," he answered.

"Oh," I mumbled. I hated sounding so naïve, but all those years of being a latch-key kid and not being allowed to hang in the streets had robbed me of a different kind of education.

"Look, I really can't leave until I get what belongs to me," he said.

"How do I know you're not going to try to attack me or kill me?" I shouted loud enough for him to get it.

"Wow! You watch a lot of television. *Law & Order?*" He cackled. "Just open up the peephole."

"No!" I shouted at him.

"I can't slip my whole body in through that small space. You really think I'm dangerous?"

"The police don't usually pin innocent men to the ground."

"Do you want to check the color of my skin again?" he joked. "Come on, I promise not to bite."

I opened the peephole to see the prettiest hazel eyes staring back at me. I stumbled back, caught off-guard by how handsome he was.

"See, I told you I'm harmless," he said, winking at me. "Here." He passed his bankcard to me. It read DAMON BRATHWAITE. "That has my name and all my money, 'cept people call me D-Waite."

"What?"

"Like D, wait up?"

"Naw, it's short for Brathwaite. Look, text that info to somebody you trust. That way if something happens to you they know who done it. I just really need to get my bag from you."

I typed in the info and sent it to Maddie, my best friend. Not only did we attend the same school, we used to live a couple of blocks away from each other until I moved here. I trusted her with my life.

She texted me back immediately: What?

I answered: Just insurance.

She typed in a confused smiley face *emoji*. I took a deep breath and opened the door. He stood there, grinning, but then his face grew serious. He reached out to me but I jumped away as if his touch burned.

"You've been crying? What's a beautiful girl like you doing crying?" He sounded genuinely concerned. "Wanna talk about it?"

"Wait here," I snapped as I hurried into my bedroom and grabbed the brown paper bag he had tossed at me. I hadn't bothered to open it and find out what it was, but suddenly like an avalanche coming out of nowhere I was pissed. I opened the bag to at least a hundred little packages of white powder. How dare this guy take a chance with my life? What if someone had seen what he had done? Couldn't I have been an accomplice to his crime? I stormed back into the living room where he stood grinning. I hurled the package over my head at him with full force, but he raised his arm and caught it before it caused any damage.

"Wait, what was that?" He seemed shocked by my actions.

"Are you kidding me? You put my life in danger throwing those drugs at me. Do I look like some drug mule? Like I'm to wind up behind bars? I don't even know you," I fumed.

"Look, I'm sorry. I wasn't thinking. I was desperate!"

"Just get out!" I yelled and felt the sting of tears in my eyes.

"I fucked up. Shit, I don't even know your name."

"Good, because I don't want to know you. Now just leave." I knew that I couldn't stop the tears and I didn't want to break down in front of him.

"I'm not leaving you like this." He took a step closer to me.

"You got what you wanted, so go!"

"No. You're hurting and I only made it worse. I'm not going to just leave you like this."

"I'm fine," I lied, fighting back tears.

"No, you're not. You can say you don't want to talk about it but please don't lie to my face."

I looked up, locking eyes with him, and before I could stop myself the floodgates opened. Tears that I thought I'd already cried let loose. Suddenly this complete stranger was holding me in his arms and comforting me. I knew that I should have separated myself and told him to leave but it just felt so good to be held. I wasn't sure how long we were there but I started feeling uncomfortable. What if he was dangerous? Clearly he was a criminal. We'd already established that.

"Dammit!" I heard myself curse as I tried to separate myself from him, except he wasn't budging. I couldn't believe how strong his arms were or how good I felt in them. *Oh no. What if he thinks this is some kind of invitation for sex?* I pushed myself away from him, wiping my face with the back of my hands. He untied the button-down shirt from around his waist and used it to dry my tears.

"I'm fine," I insisted in a voice much stronger than I intended to use.

"Really? Wow, you just not gonna let a brotha help you?" He took a step back, holding up his hands. "But you should talk about it. You can't hold all that inside. You don't ever have to see me again. Sometimes it's easier to talk to a stranger. I'm not gonna try to sell your shit to the *National Enquirer* unless it's really juicy," he teased me.

"No, it's not." I felt myself blushing.

"So spill it. You saved my ass from some serious time behind the black iron curtains so I owe you something. What's causing such a pretty little thing like you to be in so much pain? If it's your boyfriend let me know and I will set him straight."

"No. It's not a guy. I don't have a boyfriend," I confessed. I could have sworn his eyes lit up when I said that but maybe it was just my wishful thinking. I hadn't had a boyfriend yet. My mother decided that when I reached seventeen I could start to date in groups but my birthday coincided with her illness. And the last thing on my mind or hers was my love life. "My mother died two weeks ago and now I live here with my aunt," I said, but before I could finish my thought he had wrapped me in his arms again.

"You okay?" D-Waite breathed into my ear. "'Cause I could hold you all day." I couldn't stop the huge smile covering my face. "Is that a smile?" He caught me.

"No!" I tried to hide my face.

"So will you tell me your name? Please."

"It's Gabby. Gabrielle, but everybody calls me Gabby."

"Gabby, if I let you go do you promise not to hit me or scream or anything that might cause a brotha some pain?" He let me go and I backed away, embarrassed.

"Hey, there is no shame in showing your feelings. I like it. Most girls I meet spend their time tryin'a convince me that they are bulletproof."

"Bulletproof?"

"Yeah, that nothing could ever hurt them."

"Oh, yeah, I'm working on that."

"Don't. I like you like this." His eyes pierced me, and even if I wanted to I couldn't pretend he didn't affect me. I started looking around for somewhere to put my focus. "How about I go and get you something to eat? There's a bodega around the corner that makes an amazing sub. Lots of meat piled high and shit. 'Cause you look like you ain't ate in a minute."

"No, I'm all right."

"Oh, did that sound like a question? My bad. I'm going to get you some food and I'll sit here until you eat it. Uh, can I get my bankcard back?

Unless you need some cash? I'll give you the pin code." I reached into the pocket of my uniform sweater and handed him his card. "I'm coming back and you got to let me in, Gabby, okay?"

"Yes, I will let you in."

"Now lock the door behind me." He strolled out. "Lock the door," he shouted from the other side.

"Bossy." I laughed but I did as he ordered.

By the time D-Waite got back I had changed out of my uniform and into jeans and a T.

"You didn't have to dress for me," he teased as we sat down. Not only did he bring two huge subs but Lay's Barbecue chips and Mountain Dew.

I knew it should have felt weird having some strange guy—and a criminal at that—up in my place, but it didn't. I was relieved just be able to hang out with someone without them treating me like I was fragile glass about to shatter. No, this was probably the first time in a long while that I felt normal.

"Damn, girl, you can eat." His words brought me back.

"Guess I was hungry," I admitted.

"Yeah, well I'm gonna make it by business to make sure you eat."

"What's that supposed to mean?"

"I didn't stutter. I'm gonna take care of you."

"What? You don't even know me."

"Sure, I do." He pierced me with those eyes again and I knew that he wasn't playing. "Yeah, meeting you today wasn't an accident. It was fate."

"Oh really? So is this the way you seduce all the girls?"

"Not at all."

"I may be young but I'm not stupid, and I'm not that kind of girl." I stared at him, giving him more attitude than I'd ever given anyone in my life.

"I know exactly what kind of girl you are," he said, taking my hand.

I froze. It wasn't like I hadn't had crushes before or even had a boy touch my hand; it just had never felt like this. This had electricity.

"Walk me to the door. I could stay here all day with you but I can't." He grabbed his things and moved to leave. I held the door open but he pushed it closed again. "Aren't you forgetting something?"

"No." I suddenly got all shy and self-conscious.

"Look at you." D-Waite caressed my cheek. "I don't have your number." After we exchanged information it was his turn to become unsure. "Is it okay if I call you?"

"Sure, I'd like that," I said, and after I said the words I realized how much I wanted to see him again.

"And if you need anything—anything, a friend, a hug—call me."

My phone rang almost as soon as he left. I really didn't want to talk to anyone. I wanted to just lie down and think about D-Waite but I answered it anyway. "Hello!"

"Do you miss me yet?" D-Waite's cocky tone made me blush.

"No, do you miss me?" I shot back.

"Why you think I'm calling you? Wanna have lunch tomorrow? After school?"

"Sure." I knew he could see my grin through the phone.

"Good. A brotha needs something to look forward to. Now I'm sure you got homework to do."

"Ugh! Yes," I admitted.

"Get to it then."

By the time I hung up my cheeks were hurting from cheesing so hard. If you had told me a day ago that I would ever smile again I would not have believed you and now I couldn't stop myself.

3

"Wow, I didn't expect you to be cooking. You been holed up in that room since you moved in." My aunt was ten years younger than my mother and ten years older than me. For a family of black sheep she'd been the darkest. My mother had been the first person in her family to go to college, and even after she got pregnant with me she still managed to graduate on time. She gave me a pretty good life without much input from her family, until she died. She made a point to keep them out of my life since most of my relatives had gone to "camp," which was how they referred to prison life.

A couple of years ago my mother reconnected with her younger, wilder sister. Kim had been strung out on crack and worked at a strip club, and it wasn't hard to figure out that she had done a lot more than that to support her habit. She too had spent time in camp, came back to Brooklyn, and started to repair the damage to her life. I knew it wasn't easy but after my mom got sick Kim stepped up, taking care of both of us. She promised my mother than she would stay clean but I could tell it was hard, especially living so close to the crack infestation. She attended twelve-step meetings almost every day to keep her strong and sober.

"You get your homework done?" she grilled me. Even though she had never finished school she made it her mission to make sure I went to college. "Preston's on his way over. You want anything from the store?" she asked me, being sweet.

Ugh! If there was one thing I hated more than living in the projects it had to be Kim's new boyfriend, Preston. He reminded me of one of those snakes, always looking for the right moment to pounce on me. He didn't think I noticed the way his eyes always found some shit to do in my direction but of course I did. Why my aunt liked him I had no idea, but I couldn't come in here and make problems so I usually made a point to be somewhere else when he showed up. He worked as a security guard at a department store in Manhattan but he acted like he was police chief or something. It took a certain kind of person to need a job that gave them power over other people. Well, he was one of those people. I'd just finished cooking dinner when I heard the door.

"Hey, Gabby." Preston let himself into the apartment. I made a mental note that this asshole now had a key. Before he could reach where I was standing my aunt came out of her bedroom all excited to see Mr. Nothing.

"Hi. I'm gonna go into my room. Let you two have some privacy. I have some reading to do for homework," I lied.

"Stay and eat with us," Preston insisted. "Tell us what you've been up to."

"Yeah, honey, join us," my aunt chimed in.

The last thing I wanted was to sit with this jerk as he leered at me every time my aunt turned her head. My phone rang, saving me from having to plead my case.

"Hey," I spoke into the phone. "Hold on. I have to take this," I said as I excused myself.

"Does she have a boyfriend? 'Cause she seems too young to date." He gave my aunt his fake paternal concern. Like he needed to be all up in my business.

"No, she's a good girl. I don't think she's even thinking about boys yet."

"Good," the asshole added. "But I'm starting to think she don't like me. It's making me feel uncomfortable coming around." It was the last

thing I heard before going in my room and closing the door.

Maddie and I used to talk every night but
lately she'd been checking up on me more than
usual. "Hey, girl," I gushed into the phone.

"Whoa, who the hell took over my best friend?
Who is this?" she joked.

"It's me. I'm good."

"And who is Damon Braithwaite and can I
please get one?"

"Well since he doesn't have a twin I'm gonna
have to say no."

"Oh my God. You met a guy?"

"Yes!" I screamed out, giggling into the phone
just as my door swung wide open.

"Gab, come join us for dinner." My aunt stood
there hand on her hip. She didn't make it sound
like a request.

"Maddie, I'll call you back." I hung up, feeling
like a trapped animal as I followed her into the
dining area and sat down.

"So glad you changed your mind." Preston
tried to act like he hadn't made this happen. I
fixed on a fake-ass smile.

"Yeah, I want the two people I love the most
to get to know each other better." Kim was so
busy grinning up in his face she didn't notice he
hadn't taken his eyes off me.

"Your aunt and I are thinking of taking it to the next level," he boasted.

"Oh, you proposed?" I smiled as his beady eyes got all nervous darting around the room.

"Nah, that's the next next level. The two of you need a man to take care of you." He sounded all Joe Smooth but even if my aunt didn't I had his number and it was wrong. When I turned fourteen a friend's uncle gave us alcohol and tried to get us into a threesome. Ugh! Men!

"So you gonna let him move in here without getting married?" I chastised my aunt, who actually had the nerve to look shocked.

"Baby, we could use the help."

"I'm only here for six months at the most. Can't you wait until then?" I pleaded with her.

"Baby girl, don't I deserve to be happy?'

"If it's so real what difference is six months?"

"We're the adults and you're the child. You don't get a vote," he said in a threatening voice.

I jumped up and stormed into my room. I was pissed and just wanted to be left alone. But of course that too proved impossible.

"Hey, baby girl." Preston opened my door without bothering to knock. "I know you been through a lot lately so I'm gonna excuse your bad attitude this time. We just need to get to know each other a little better. You'll see that I'll be

real good to you and to your aunt." He came over
to the bed and stared down at me.

"Gabby, the nicer you are to me the nicer I can
be to you." He turned and walked out, leaving
my door wide open.

4

Maddie grabbed me as soon as I got to my locker. Clearly she'd been waiting for me to show up. Of course in six years of friendship we'd rarely kept anything from each other, even her mother's affair two years ago, which had threatened her parents' marriage.

"So tell me."

"Nothing to really tell. Yet." I grinned not able to contain myself.

"That don't look like nothing on your face."

"Fine. He's this guy that I guess lives near my aunt."

"So what school does he go to?'

"I don't know."

"He docs go to school?"

"Why does that matter?" I snapped.

"Gab, the plan was that you were going to live with your aunt, and wait for our acceptance letters from Harvard so we can be roommates. You can't go getting involved with those people."

"What people?"

"People who don't have a plan. Those who aren't interested in forward movement and changing the world. People like us."

"Like us how? Maddie, we're not so alike. You live in a multimillion-dollar brownstone with two parents—one's an attorney—an unlimited credit card, country homes, winter ski trips, and vacations abroad. How are we alike?"

"Ouch! So what? Now you're playing the underprivileged card, Gab?"

"I'm not playing anything. I'm just speaking the truth."

"Well I don't like this guy already."

"Yeah, I'm not so sure he'd be a big fan of yours either." We stared at each other for way too long. Neither of us was budging. Finally she broke the silence.

"I know you're going through some stuff but I'm not the enemy."

"Shit, I know. It's just . . ." I didn't have to finish. That's the way it had always been with us but I couldn't bring myself to tell her that our differences had gotten a whole lot bigger than money and location.

I managed to avoid Maddie the rest of the day by working on my science paper in the library at lunch. I hurried out of school when the bell rang. All I wanted was to see D-Waite and, well, I didn't know what but I was sure that just being with him would make me feel better. He hadn't called me or mentioned where we would meet so I was surprised to see him waiting at my bus stop when I stepped off the B54.

"Hey, pretty." He came up to me with the biggest grin on his face.

"Hey." I suddenly felt shy.

"Let me have that." He reached for my heavy backpack, slinging it over one shoulder. "What they teaching you in that school? Everything?"

"More. You're not trying to hide any more of your stuff in my bag are you?"

"Nope, I'm all clean." He grabbed my hand, leading me across the Fort Green Park to the nicer neighborhood of Clinton Hill. D-Waite took me to a small café a few blocks but worlds away from the hood. They seemed to know him when they took our order.

"So what? This is where you bring your dates?"

"No. I don't usually date."

"Wow! Now that's a line."

"Let me get something straight: I'm not above lying. I have done it plenty, especially to save my ass, but I like you and I haven't lied to you and I'm not planning on lying to you." He pierced me with those beautiful eyes and I felt myself going all jelly.

"So I can ask you anything and you'll tell me the truth?"

"Just be careful you want the answers."

"Why are you dealing drugs and not in school?"

"'Cause I learned early that you have to play the hand you been dealt. I had to have my back early and, well, that meant figuring out how to survive and I did."

"You ever think about getting out?"

"Every day!" He had an expression on his face that I couldn't quite read.

"What?"

"I reserve the right to be more than a stereotype."

"Me too," I added.

By the time we finished eating and he walked me back across the park it seemed like we'd known each other a lot longer than twenty-four hours. I was so distracted by the easy time we were having that I hadn't noticed the police car stopped in front of us. D-Waite dropping my hand was the first sign that something was up. One short Italian guy and a big black guy policeman got out of the car and approached us. D-Waite stood in front of me protectively.

"D-Waite. I see you been busy." The black cop stared menacingly at him.

"Young lady, you need to be more careful about the company you keep." His partner focused on me.

"What's in the bag?"

"Books, my laptop, homework," I chimed in.

"Humph, using a schoolgirl to transport your drugs. Hand over the bag."

"On what grounds?" I stepped in. "This seems like harassment. We weren't doing anything that would give you cause to search my bag."

"You're conspiring with a known drug dealer."

"Thompson, leave her alone. She's innocent."

"Until proven guilty? Just being with you makes her guilty."

"Just let her go." D-Waite handed me my bag. "You can mess with me but leave her out of it."

"Whoa! And they say chivalry is dead. Guess we found it alive and well in Brooklyn." A sound on their radio got their attention. The Italian cop nodded to the other one toward their car.

"We're gonna let this one pass; but if I were you, young lady, I'd stick to the books." The cops got back in their car and headed off.

This time I was the one who grabbed D-Waite's hand. We were silent as we walked the rest of the way to my building. Outside my building D-Waite stopped and turned to me.

"Remember I said that I don't date? Now do you understand why?"

"So you do want to date me?" I joked but he looked serious. Really serious.

"Gabby?"

"Fine. If you don't like me then good to know now," I snapped, and then stormed away before he could see the tears welling up in my eyes. Only instead of him leaving he followed me. He took hold of my hand.

"D-Waite!"

I turned to see Mika and her girls stomping toward us. Shit, this was all I needed. I wanted to run but with him holding my hand it was impossible.

"Mika, I'm kind of busy right now."

"You weren't too busy two nights ago when you were all up inside of me. What you tryin'a get you, a little bit of that uptight schoolgirl?"

"Mika, I said I'm busy." He dismissed her.

"Yeah, well the next time you want your dick sucked I'ma be too busy too. Go on with that little bitch then." She shot me a look that caused me to groan inwardly. If I thought that girl hated me before, I was now in total enemy territory.

"Get off me." I snatched my arm away from D-Waite and ran into the building. But by the time I reached my front door he was waiting for me, breathing heavy, like he had run all the way up five flights of stairs.

"Why are you here? You already told me that you didn't want to date me and now that I know you're fucking that girl I don't want to date you either." I sneered at him.

"Gabby, come on. You know I like you."

"Whatever! I don't like you." I folded my arms over my chest.

"I asked you not to do that. We promised not to lie to each other."

"I'm not lying to you," I lied.

"So you don't like me as much as I like you?" He got so close I swore he could hear my heartbeat.

"So what? You're sleeping with Mika? She hates me."

"She hates everybody."

"Not you apparently."

"Ugh!" He let out a growl, slapping his hands against the wall. "Mika is different. She's not like you. To her, sex and men, it's all casual and no big deal."

"And you believe that? It's a big deal to everybody. I got friends who hook up and then call me crying 'cause they really like the guy. Sex is always a big deal."

"And you know that personally?" He looked wounded just asking me the question.

"It's none of your business!" I glared at him, and before I knew it he was pressed against me, pinning my body to the wall.

"Yes, it is my business because you are my business." And then his lips were on me, crushing me, and before I could stop myself I was kissing him back; and it wasn't no PG kiss like I'd had with other boys. This was a grown-ass passionate kiss. My first. I felt a hunger and longing shoot all the way down to my vagina. I couldn't stop it and I didn't want to. Finally he wrenched himself back, grabbing his hair in his hands.

"I can't afford to feel this way!" he raged, staring at me with undisguised angst.

"Then fine. Leave. If that's what you want. Leave."

He turned and pounced on me again, kissing me all over my face and lips and letting me know that this was real and that I wasn't alone with my feelings.

"I can't, Gabby. Fuck! I can't," he cried.

"Then what are you going to do?"

"I don't know. I just don't know. You may not lie but I don't play games."

I pushed him away, struggling to locate my keys in my bag. "Then leave me alone until you know." I grabbed my keys and put them in the door just as someone snatched it open. Preston stood there, staring at the both of us.

"What's going on?" He shot D-Waite a hostile glare.

"Nothing," I shot out as I raced past him into my room.

Preston slammed the door and followed me.

"Who was that guy?"

"Nobody." I opened my bag and pulled out my books and my computer.

"You wanna have a drink? Talk?"

"I have homework and I need to study for a test." I picked up my phone. "It's a project with a friend."

"Well your aunt is working late so I told her I would cook dinner."

"I just ate." I started pushing buttons, pretending to call someone, but my phone started ringing. I answered on the first ring. "Hello?"

Preston stood there like he was waiting for something.

"Hold on," I spoke into the phone. "Yes?" I glanced up at Preston. "Anything else?"

"Nah, I'll be out here if you need anything." He looked disappointed as he left. I got up and closed the door, making a mental note to put a lock on it.

5

I was so busy hurrying through that morning fog to get to the bus stop that I hadn't noticed the four girls coming straight at me until it was too late.

"Fuck you think you're going?" Mika sneered so close to my face I could smell her bad morning breath.

I tried to take a step back but one of the other girls had closed me in. In fact there was one on all four sides of me. "I'm going to school."

"Yeah? Why bother? 'Cause they ain't teaching you the right shit," spoke out a heavyset girl wearing a bad weave and the wrong clothes for her figure.

"Naynay, you got that shit right." A short, petite girl wearing braids and a scowl poked me at my side.

"Excuse me. I can't miss my bus." I tried to maneuver away from them but they only pressed against me tighter.

"I can't miss my bus," the one behind me mimicked me but I couldn't see her face.

"What you think, you some white girl? Going to that fancy-ass school?" Mika accused me.

"No, I just want to get an education." I knew I shouldn't have antagonized them.

"And you saying we don't, bitch?" Mika snapped.

"No, I'm not saying that, but I can't be late." I could hear the fear in my voice. Being late scared me because I knew my teacher would send me the office, where everyone would hound me to talk about my feelings. But I was definitely more afraid of what these girls would do to me. "I just don't want any trouble."

"You should have thought about that shit." Naynay spat the words out at me.

"Yeah, when you stepped on my territory you were looking for trouble."

"No, I wasn't. I just moved here." I could hear myself pleading with them. I'd been hating God for taking my mother but I started praying I'd get out of there alive.

"I'm not talking that kind of location. What, you tryin'a act stupid? Tryin'a piss me the fuck off?" Mika poked her fingertip against my forehead. I must have looked as confused as I felt.

"She act like she don't know what the fuck I'm talking about. All that school and you still a dumb bitch."

"I got to go." I tried to push through the human wall they'd built around me but they were stronger and more determined.

"She's talking about D-Waite," the voice behind me shouted, her hot breath stinging my ear. I felt my stomach do flip-flops at the mention of his name. It actually hurt to hear it out loud.

"Yeah, you can't come into our hood, stealing our men. You may look like some innocent-ass schoolgirl but maybe that's just your stripper act." Naynay glared at me.

"Look, I don't want any trouble."

"Then you need to step the fuck off and keep your ass away from her man." Hot breath seethed in my ear.

"So he's your boyfriend?" I spoke directly to Mika, who didn't hide her surprise at my question.

"No, he's not my boyfriend," she mocked me. "We're fuck buddies and I plan to keep on fucking him so I don't need no stuck-up bitch cock blocking me."

I had never heard the term "cock blocking" but I had a pretty good idea what she meant.

"Then you don't have to worry because I'm not planning to have sex with D-Waite."

"Bitch, who you calling worried? I'm just letting you know that you need to watch your back before I watch it for you."

"That's right, bitch," Miss Hot Breath screamed in my ear before banging her fists on my back.

"Hey! Get away from her," a familiar male voice screamed out. It caused them to back away.

"You better watch yourself!" Naynay kicked me in the butt and raced off to join the others.

"You all right?" Preston came up to me.

"I'm fine." I kept moving toward the bus stop.

"Yeah, well whatever you did to piss those hoodrats off you need to stop it. I'm not always gonna be here to rescue you."

"I didn't ask for you to rescue me!" I snapped, stomping away, but he stayed on my heels.

"Yeah, well anybody could see those girls meant business. This ain't Brooklyn Heights or Park Slope. These girls don't play by no rules. They will hurt you and not think twice."

"I can handle myself."

"Yeah, I see that. I can be an important ally to you, Gabby. People respect me. All I need to do is put the word out and nobody will bother you.

I told you that you need a man to look out for you."

"Aren't you supposed to be looking out for my aunt?" I couldn't help glaring.

"I am looking out for her! But that don't mean I can't look out for you too."

"I'm good. Gotta go." I took off racing to catch the bus coming up the street.

"Gabby!"

I turned to see D-Waite bopping up the block from the other direction. I could see Preston watching out the corner of my eyes. I didn't dare swivel all the way around to see if Mika and her girls were close by. I raced right past D-Waite. For a moment our eyes locked and I could have sworn I saw hurt in his eyes. Maybe it was my imagination because I desperately wanted to believe that I wasn't the only one affected after our time together, that it was the one part of my life that had given me hope in the last couple of days.

I got on the bus and squeezed all the way to the back just to catch the smallest glimpse of his head. I turned and looked out the window to find Preston watching me watch D-Waite, a hostile stare on his face.

6

Mrs. Sharzer sat across from me, reviewing some papers, her thin lips pressed together. I knew that eventually she would turn her focus on me but, man, was I wanting this to be over.

"Gabrielle, I wanted you to know that a few of the schools have already called to see what your first choice school is. They all seem to want to offer you some sort of financial package. But even with a full-ride scholarship you're still going to need some financial support. We just found out that your mother's insurance policy wasn't current. Because of your situation we have made the allowance and allowed you to stay in school and graduate, but it may be necessary for you to look into some kind of employment. How are you doing? Your teachers have been worried about you."

"I'm good," I lied just desperate to get out of there.

"Because you are important to all of us at St. Agnes. I need you to know that whatever you need, we are your family. We're here for you." She wrung her anorexic hands and offered me a supportive smile.

All I could think was, *can I come live in your beautiful house where I wouldn't be accosted by bullies or a lecherous older man angling to be my first?* But instead I just smiled, playing along, and nodded as if I believed her.

"Ugh!" I exited to find Maddie waiting for me. She stuck two fingers in her mouth and pretended to gag.

"Right? All this fake concern is making me feel soooo loved." I laughed.

"Well just to balance that shit out, I don't give a shit."

"Nice."

"Wanna come over and do homework?" she asked and the thought of avoiding Mika and her crew made me jump at the offer. Not to mention Preston. I could probably spend the night if I played it right.

We got our stuff and headed out. There, leaning against a car parked on the curb, was D-Waite. My face must have lit up like a Christmas tree by the look on Maddie's face.

"Who is that total hottie? Got you all wide open?" she teased.

"Shhh! I wanna act cool," I warned her.

"Late for that. He's got that same goofy look on his face."

"Hey." I approached D-Waite.

"Hey." He grinned at me. Maddie cleared her throat, breaking us out of our embarrassing daze.

"D-Waite, this is my friend Maddie."

"Best friend Maddie," she said with total attitude. "So what brings you to our prison?" she joked.

"I wanted to make sure my girl got home safe."

"Well we were going to go to—"

I kneed her before she could say anything more. "So, Mads, let's get together tomorrow?" I raised my eyes at her, hoping she'd go along with me.

"Later, Gab," she snapped and stormed off in a huff.

Damn, I just couldn't catch a break today, but I really wanted to hang out with D-Waite. He had just called me his girl.

"You need to go after her?" he asked.

I glanced down the street after an angry Maddie and decided to move in the other direction. D-Waite followed me.

"Nah, it's good. So what are you doing here? I mean you told me that you didn't want to date me."

"I wanted to see you."

"For what? To tell me again that you can't afford to have feelings for me?"

"Do you know what I would do if anything happened to you? I'm not there all the time. I may not be able to protect you."

"Nobody can protect anybody all the time. Not a parent or a husband or even the cops. Life doesn't work that way."

"I know." His words came out like a wounded animal. "But I done seen some shit and been through things and it's not pretty. My life is different than yours."

"I cleaned up my mother's vomit and stood by as she died. You tryin'a tell me I've led some sheltered life? I have a father who I heard wants nothing to do with me and I'm living with my aunt and . . ." I let it drop off, not ready to say out loud what had become painfully clear.

"What? Tell me?"

"Nothing. It's nothing." I turned my head away, avoiding his eyes.

"Gabby, what are you not telling? We promised not to lie to each other." He grabbed me by the hand and turned me to face him.

"There is no 'we.' You already made that clear and you haven't told me one thing that would make me think differently."

"I'm falling for you. I can't stop thinking about you. I can't sleep or eat. I just want to be with you all the time." He finished. I let out an exasperated breath.

"And?"

"And this kind of shit doesn't happen to me."

"So, what, you Superman or some shit?" I couldn't stop myself from smiling.

"No, baby girl, I ain't Superman, but if that's who you want me to be then I damn sure want to try." He focused all of his attention on me. I felt my knees getting weak. He stopped me and wrapped one arm around my waist, pulling me closer to him.

"Ahh!" I took a sharp intake of breath, feeling overwhelmed and heady. This wasn't the kind of thing that happened to me either.

"What are you doing to me?" His voice lost its edge.

"The same thing you're doing to me," I said all breathy and girly.

"You ever play cards?"

"Spades, with my aunt."

"There's a gambling term that means you're willing to risk your entire pot. It's called being all in. Do you know what that means?" He stared down at me, his eyes emotional and exposed.

"Yes," I answered, suddenly afraid to move, to break the moment.

"Well, with you I'm all in."

"Are you serious?"

"What do you think, Gab?"

"I think I'm all in too."

And he held my chin up and planted the deepest, most intense kiss on me. This was even different from the kiss yesterday. It was just as strong and probing but without the agony of a man trying to run away. This was the kiss of a man who was exactly where he wanted to be.

"You hungry?"

"No. I don't have an appetite . . . for food." I stared at him.

"Girl, you gonna get yourself in trouble you keep looking at me like that."

"Is that a promise?" I flirted, breaking into an even bigger smile.

He took my backpack, then my hand, and led me to the Brooklyn promenade. For the next ninety minutes it felt like we were the only two people on the planet and that was fine with me, until D-Waite's phone started ringing, dragging us back into the world.

"Yeah, nah. Fuck! Yeah, I got this. I said I got this!" he shouted at whoever was on the other end before hanging up. He grabbed my hand and almost dragged me down the street.

"Whoa!" I snatched my hand out of his and stopped walking.

"Gabby, we got to go. This is serious. Fuck!" He looked really worried.

"What is it? What happened, D-Waite?"

"I can't tell you."

"Of course you can. I'm not a baby!" I said like I was having a tantrum, stomping my foot.

"I'm not saying that but this shit is not play. The people I deal with are either so desperate for what I have they will kill each other to get it, or so dangerous that if something goes wrong they will have no problem killing me." The weight of his words and the fear in his eyes made me scared for him. He stepped off the street and hailed a cab. *This must be really serious,* I thought.

"I'm sorry," I mumbled as a taxi stopped in front of us.

"Thank you." He opened the door and let me get in first.

"Cumberland housing projects on Myrtle," he directed the cabby. I snuggled close to him as the car took off.

Within minutes we had arrived one block from my aunt's house. D-Waite paid and hurried me out of the cab. A big-body SUV sat at the curb in front of us. Two huge muscle-bound guys got out of the car and stopped D-Waite as we passed.

One stood right in his path and snatched his arm.

"Let's go, D-Waite." I gripped his hand.

"Go home. I'll call you later." He gave me a look that made me listen to him, even though I didn't want to leave him with those guys. I hurried down the street and when I turned I saw them shoving him into the SUV.

7

"Where you been?" my aunt questioned me the moment I stepped into the apartment.

"Just hanging out with a friend."

"A friend from school?" She stared at me.

"No. I thought you were going to be at your meeting."

"I didn't go tonight. I was tired. Preston said he saw you with one of these little hoodlums. Gab, these boys around here ain't like the ones you used to in that fancy school. They will say anything and do anything to get what they want and after they get it they will pass you on to one of their friends."

"That sounds just like my high school. It's no different over there."

"I thought you would learn from your mother's mistake. These boys around here ain't gonna do shit but leave you knocked up and on welfare."

"What do you mean my mother's mistake? You mean me?"

"No, that's not what I'm saying. She had dreams for her future and once she had you she turned all those dreams into dreams for you. You don't want to let her down. She gave up everything to make sure you had a future. You willing to throw that away for someone with no future?"

"And how am I doing that? I'm going to school and getting good grades."

"Yes, but you are also judged by the company you keep. Just being seen with that kind of boy can get you in trouble in this neighborhood." The last thing I wanted her to find out now was about my run-in with Mika. Of course Preston would probably run and tell her anyway with his big-ass mouth.

"And does that apply to you or just me?"

"What's that supposed to mean?"

I didn't say anything. I knew I had said more than I should.

"So you talking about Preston?"

I turned away so she couldn't see the look of pure disgust on my face at the mention of his name.

"You got something to say then say it."

"No, I don't have anything to say. I need to do my homework."

"What do you have against Preston? He thinks you don't like him."

"I don't."

"Look, I know that your mother never dated. Preston said that's what it's about. You're not used to having men around or sharing the adults in your life. The women."

"Oh, and what do you think, Auntie?"

"Gabby, I don't know what the hell to think. This mother-aunt thing is new to me. I ain't never had to think about anybody other than myself but I like him. You don't know how hard it is once you done all the things I done to have a decent man give a shit about you. And he wants to be committed."

"Moving in is not a commitment. It's just a change of address for him. I think you can do better."

"Well I been out there and I don't. He loves me."

"Then why isn't he trying to marry you? He's taking you off the market for free."

"What do you know about grown-folk business? You been so sheltered you believe everything you see on television."

"This is 2013. I don't live under a rock. I got social media, friends, and eyes and ears. I know a lot more than you think. I seen all kinds of things. Just because people have good jobs and money don't mean they're not as messed up as poor people. You can't shelter anybody anymore."

"Well, I just need you to give Preston a break."

"I need you to let me put a lock on my door. I need some privacy."

"Fine."

"Wait. What did you mean about my father being from around here? I thought they met when my mother was in college."

"She was in college. He was slinging drugs on the avenue."

"My father was a drug dealer?"

"Yeah. Ain't that a good enough reason not to get all messed up with one?"

"Is that why he wanted nothing to do with me?"

"What?" She seemed genuinely confused. "Your mother didn't tell him about you. I don't think he even knows that he has a child."

"She lied to me? She made it seem like he was the one who had rejected me. That she had no choice but to raise me on her own."

"Maybe that's how she felt because of what he did for a living."

"What else do you know about my father?"

"I can't talk to you about this. Your mother wouldn't like it."

"You already told me more than she ever did. Besides, my mother is dead. I'm seventeen years old and I don't want to be treated like I'm some baby."

"Big John Thompson was a legend around here. He owned the streets. Hell, the first time I ever got high was off-a some weed from one of his crew. I think because he was in love with your mother he always had a soft spot for me. Treated me real good, but once he went away the dealers who took over his territory didn't give a shit about nobody. They were all about stacking paper by whatever means necessary."

"My father was a drug dealer? What happened to him?"

"I think he's upstate somewhere."

"Hey, ladies." I hadn't even heard the door open when Preston entered the apartment. My head was swirling with all this new information. My mother had been lying to me all these years. I grabbed my bag and headed into my room.

"Don't walk out of here without saying hello," I heard Preston yell after me.

"Let her go." My aunt actually sounded worried. "She finally heard the truth."

"About what?" Preston asked. I closed my door, not wanting to hear the rest of their conversation about me.

I opened my computer and logged on. I needed to get more information about my father. All it took was a few clicks to catch up on the man I knew nothing about ten minutes ago. Big John Thompson was one of the key drug dealers taken down in a sting thirteen years ago. A photo of him popped up on my computer. I expanded the image and looked for similarities between us. I guessed we had the same eyes, and I did see a resemblance in the shape of our faces. God this felt weird that after all these years of not knowing here I was looking into the eyes of my father. He was handsome and I could see why my mother would find him attractive.

I wanted to call Maddie and tell her, but did I really want to share that my father was a convicted felon in prison for selling drugs to children? It said that he was doing twenty-five years to life. Did that mean he'd never get out of prison? That I'd never meet him? Apparently he'd earned a small fortune from his drug dealing but a large part of his assets were never recovered. It had something to do with off-shore accounts and the government not being able to confiscate his property. I guessed Big John was smarter than they expected.

Should I write him a letter and identify myself or should I pretend that he doesn't exist? Could I even go back to the way it was before? I grabbed my phone to call D-Waite. He would know what to do, but I couldn't call him. Not yet. He had his own trouble to deal with. And that was worrying me even more. I picked up the phone and called Maddie. I didn't know what I wanted to talk about but I needed to hear a familiar and safe voice.

"Hey, I'm sorry about today."

"You mean dumping me for that hoodlum? What are you doing messing around with some-one like him?"

"You don't know anything about him!" I defended D-Waite.

"I know that you and he have nothing in common."

"We have more in common than you and I ever will."

"What, because you're both black? Really, Gab?"

"No, because we just do," I argued.

"I got to go." Maddie hung up the phone on me.

It wasn't the first time we'd disagreed about things but something about this was different. I felt more alone than ever. I clicked back on the computer and stared at the picture of my father. Maybe I wasn't as alone as I thought.

8

I slipped out the door and down the stairs. It was late, but D-Waite called and said he was downstairs and I needed to talk to him. I could tell he wasn't one of those guys who liked to really talk on the phone so I came out to meet him.

"Hey, baby." He took my hand and smiled down at me.

"You all right?"

"Oh, earlier? Yeah. It was actually a good thing."

"What happened?" I asked and he gave me that look that said this was off-limits. "Fine. Keep secrets."

"It's not a secret. You know what you need to know and nothing more." He leaned over and kissed me. We were both so busy grinning that neither of us noticed the guy on the bike.

"Damn, boy, you acting straight-up sprung out holding some bitch's hand." A guy with his hair in cornrows braided back rode his bike around us in circles.

"Go on, man, and stop playing," D-Waite joked so I knew that this must be a friend of his.

"What, you gon' be all rude and shit? No intros?"

"Well I'm thinking since you called my girl a bitch you don't deserve to meet her."

"My bad. You know how I get down."

"Gabby, this is Taj. And Taj, Gabby."

"Hey, Gabby. What's up? I ain't used to seeing my boy holding hands like in some PG movie."

"Good-bye, Taj."

"Folks are hanging in the park. Y'all wanna go?"

"Nah. Later, man."

"We might come," I threw out there.

"A'ight," he said before popping a wheelie and rolling away on his bike.

"Oh, we might? That ain't never gonna happen," D-Waite scolded me.

"So you can hang out but I can't?"

"I don't want you around people like that."

"People like what?"

"You know what I mean."

"And what? I'm some fine china who can't hang out with your friends?"

"You don't know what they're like. They can be dangerous."

"Maybe I'm not who you think I am. You ever heard of Big John Thomson?"

"Hell yeah! Everybody knows Big John. He's no joke. He recruited the guys I work for. Word is even though he's incarcerated he's not out of the game. They say he knows everything that goes down in these streets."

"Well, he's my father. So I'm not as precious as you thought."

"You shitting me?" His eyes were big like saucers.

"No. I'm not shitting you. Big John is the other half of my DNA."

"Wow! What is he like?" He was almost jumping out of his skin with excitement.

I had to glance away when I answered because I felt the tears stinging my eyes. "I've never met him," I admitted.

"Oh, yeah, you said he wanted nothing to do with you? Baby, I'm sorry."

"Well I'm not so sure about that," I said as the hugeness of the revelation hit me in the stomach. I must have looked the way I felt because the next thing I knew D-Waite had his arms around me, comforting me.

"Baby. Talk to me."

"My mother lied to me. She didn't even want me to know that he's my father."

"Are you sure?"

"Yes. They were together all during high school and when she was in college they hooked up and she got pregnant. Not even that original."

"And she never told him?"

"No."

"So what are you going to do? I mean he's a huge deal."

"I want to dedicate my life to putting people like him away. To make the streets safe for kids again."

"Safe from people like me?" He stared at me.

I leaned in and kissed him. I didn't have all the answers but the one thing that I had become sure about was that I needed him in my life.

"I will take that as a no." He laughed, clearly relieved. "Let's go." He took my hand and led me down the street.

"So we're going to the park?"

"No!"

"But where?"

"Just trust me." He squeezed my hand.

We crossed the street and cut through the park to the other side of Fort Greene. The upwardly mobile side where it had once been mostly Blacks had now gentrified us into the minorities. He stopped and glanced around as if he was afraid we were being followed. Then we moved a few doors up Portland Avenue to a renovated four-story brownstone. We climbed the stairs and he unlocked the door. We ducked into the lobby, then went through another door and up a single flight of stairs. When he opened the door to an apartment, I didn't know what I was expecting but this wasn't it. The tastefully furnished one-bedroom apartment could have been on Maddie's block. It was an advertisement for Pottery Barn and the Apple Store.

"What is this place?"

"It's mine." He couldn't contain the pride in his voice.

"But I thought you lived in the projects."

"Everybody thinks I do. I have a place there but this is my home."

"So what? It's your love shack?"

"Nah, you the only person I've ever brought here. But since I'm falling in love with you it can be our love shack," he joked.

I took a tour around. "I love this place."

"Me too. That's why I keep it private. I just don't want folks up in here."

"What's this?" I walked over and picked up a guitar. "You play?"

"Yeah, and I write songs."

"So you're a musician?"

"I guess but . . ." Then he stopped.

"But what?"

"I just do what I do."

"Can I ask you something?" He nodded, so I continued, "How come since you're obviously smart and able to pull this off . . ."

"I'm not in college? Or trying to make it as a musician?"

"Yeah."

"I felt like I had to get out there and hustle for mine. I didn't grow up with a lot of options and when I finally got some I didn't trust them. I didn't have anyone."

"Well you do now." I stepped close to him. For a long time we just stood there staring at each other.

"Cool."

"When I go to college maybe you can move to Boston with me."

"Boston! And do what?"

"College, music, me." I planted a deep, wet kiss on him.

"This real?" he questioned me.

"It is for me," I answered, meaning every word.

"Me too." And we fell into each other's arms, kissing and touching as if our bodies couldn't get close enough. This felt crazy and wonderful and scary but mostly it felt right. I leaned against him, feeling his manhood growing to full size. At least I hoped it was because it was rock hard and huge. He led me over to the couch and laid me down. He kneeled down next to me, lifted up my skirt, and started kissing my stomach, working his way down my body.

"Aaah." A gasp escaped from my mouth. I felt on fire with a desire I had never had before. This was what all the girls at school were whispering about, the reason they kept hooking up with guys who treated them like shit and never bothered to call them back or acknowledge them in public. Oh, damn I wanted him to show me everything that I had been missing. He took my pants off and let them drop to the floor. His hand lifted the band of my underwear and kept traveling until his fingers starting rubbing against my pubic hair. I started thrashing around, arching my back, lifting my butt cheeks off the couch.

"Wow! You're wet." He sighed as his fingers slipped inside of me. I writhed around, dancing on his fingers as they manipulated me until I felt like I was about to pee on myself. I jumped up, pushing him away.

"What?" He looked wounded by my reaction.

"I . . . I don't . . . I was about to pee on myself," I confessed, feeling completely humiliated. He burst out laughing, looking almost relieved.

"It's not funny!" I threw one of the couch pillows at him.

"Oh yes, it is. You've never had an orgasm." He reached out to me; his voice became soft as he enveloped me in his arms. "Gabby, have you ever done this before?" I dropped my face into my hands, avoiding his gaze. "So nobody has ever given you an orgasm?" The shocked expression on my face said it all. Now it was his turn to be surprised.

"You've never done it before?" My silence confirmed his question. "Never?" If I had been one shade lighter I would have been a bright shade of red. Luckily the melanin protected me from looking more embarrassed.

"Have you even kissed a guy before?"

"Yes." I frowned at him. He didn't have to make it seem so weird. There were guys who tried but I always wanted to wait for the right one. They all seemed so inexperienced and awkward or else like they were watching so much online porn that they were dying to shove you into some role and pretend they cared about your satisfaction.

"But nothing more?"

"No," I admitted and wanted to melt into the couch.

"Oh, baby." He kissed me on the neck. "We need to slow this way down."

"No!" I balked.

"But, Gab, you have no idea what this means."

"Why does it have to mean anything? You have sex with Mika all the time. What does that mean?"

"It doesn't mean much but Mika's different."

"No, she's not. She's a girl you have sex with and I'm a girl you won't have sex with. Right now I would rather be her than me!" I stood up, putting my clothes back on.

"Don't say that."

"Why? If she were here and not me you would fuck her!"

"But sex don't mean the same thing for her. She's slept with so many guys I'm just one of many, but you're a virgin." His words made it sound like some disease.

"Well I'm sorry I'm not as experienced as your other girls. I'll go and fuck a bunch of guys and after I'm experienced I'm sure you'll want to fuck me." I laced up my sneakers, anxious to get out of there with an ounce of my dignity.

"Is that what you think? That I don't want you? Girl, you can't be more wrong. I want you. I want you in a way that I have never wanted anyone in my life." He smashed his lips against mine; his hunger and need matched mine.

9

The bright sunlight jarred me awake. I opened my eyes and waited to adjust to the daylight. At first I was disoriented, forgetting where I was, but one look at the beautiful man lying next to me brought it all back. Then I realized something else. I was gonna be late to school, but I had to face my aunt and Preston first. How the hell was I gonna explain where I had spent the night and with whom? I jumped up, threw on my clothes, and tried not to wake D-Waite.

"Hey!" His sleepy-sounding voice made me want to crawl back under the covers and snuggle.

"Hey, yourself. I gotta run."

"You in trouble?" he asked but I could only shrug my shoulders. Had it been my mother I would probably be grounded for life, but my aunt was barely ten years older than me. Still, I had to get my butt out of there before the shit hit the fan.

D-Waite got up and took something out of a box on the mantle. "Come here." He motioned me to him. He hugged me. "It's gonna be all right."

"I know," I answered softly.

"Here." He pressed a set of keys into my hand. "What's this?"

"I want this to be our place. You can come here anytime you want. Just be careful you're not followed."

"All right." A huge smile spread across my face.

"I'm serious about you."

"I know; now let me get out of here so that I can get to school."

He gave me a kiss good-bye and I left. I shoved the keys in my pocket and raced down the stairs, checking to make sure I wasn't being watched. I passed a few white people heading off to work. I picked up the pace as I crossed the park. It made sense that the first person I would see was Mika but unlike last time she was walking alone. Her mouth stretched into an angry line as she shot daggers at me. I made a point to give her lots of room as I hurried past her. I ain't gonna lie, I was afraid that she would follow me, but she didn't. By the time I got into the apartment my heart had stopped racing. I almost reached my bedroom when Preston stepped into the hallway, shirtless.

"Where the hell you been all night?" he screamed at me.

"I was with my friend. Excuse me, I have to get to school." I took a step but he didn't budge.

"What friend, Gabby?" he challenged me.

"My friend Maddie," I lied.

"So I'm supposed to believe you were with some girlfriend all night?"

"I don't care what you believe. You're not my guardian. I don't have to answer to you."

"Oh, so you a bad bitch now?" He got up in my face.

"I am not your problem. Why are you bothering me?"

"Somebody has to make sure that you don't wind up like your mother getting knocked up by some drug dealer. Yeah, I said it. Or like your aunt giving blowjobs for chump change just so she could buy drugs."

"Get away from me," I shouted.

"Or what? What you gonna do?"

"I don't know. Call the police. Report you."

"And you think that's gonna help your aunt? Without me to protect her she would be back on rocks doing anything to get high. That what you want? For your aunt to be cracked out again so that you become a ward of the state?"

"What do you want?" I yelled with undisguised hatred.

"I want you to start treating me with respect. No. I want you to be real nice to me." He reached out and put his hand on my waist.

I reacted, pushing it away. "Don't ever put your hand on me," I screamed.

"Feisty!" He licked his lips and lunged for me. Before I could get away he grabbed me and snatched me close. Way too close for my comfort.

"Get off of me!" I screamed. "I'm telling my aunt. You fucking pervert!"

"You say one fucking thing I will break your little ass into two pieces. What would I want to do with you when I can have a grown-ass woman who knows how to handle her man like a pro?"

"Touch me and I will send you to jail," I promised, my voice razor sharp.

That got him to let me go. I raced into my room and shut the door. My breathing was so heavy I had to sit down to stop myself from throwing up. *Fuck! This should have been a great day for me but instead I'm fighting off my aunt's horny boyfriend.*

When I came out in my uniform Preston was standing next to the door, waiting for me. I took a step back.

"Gabby, you need to calm down and keep this shit to yourself."

"Whatever!" I snapped. The only thing I wanted was to get out of there and away from him.

"I was kidding!" His voice took on more of an edge. He took hold of my elbow and bent my arm behind my back.

"Ouch!" I yelled out in pain. "That hurts."

"It will hurt a lot more if you go telling your aunt lies. You understand that?" He let me go and I took off and raced out the door, my heart beating a mile a minute.

10

I wasn't sure how I got through the school day after the drama with Preston. I had to figure out a way to avoid him. I really didn't want to cause my aunt any hurt or lead her into a relapse, but I wasn't sure that staying quiet about her psycho boyfriend would be much helping her either. If it weren't for D-Waite I would be hating my new life but instead he had become my everything. At the moment he was everything.

Maddie walked by me without speaking and then at lunchtime she actually sat with the popular girls, who we thought were shallow. There were so many things about this new life I wasn't willing to share with her. Until my mother died Maddie and I had never had a secret. We shared everything. I guess it's called growing up, but after last night I didn't feel like the same person. Something had definitely changed and I wasn't ready to share the details with anyone.

At first D-Waite refused to make love to me. He kept saying that we needed to wait, that he wanted me to be sure. I tried telling him that I had never been so sure about anything in my life, but he wasn't buying it. He kept pushing me away and attempting to make me feel better with kisses, but I had made up he was the one and that that night was the night for it to happen.

"Gabby, you don't know what this means." *He kept trying to talk me out of it.*

"Means to who? Me or you?"

"This can change your whole life."

"I'm not stupid. I may be a virgin but I know about protection."

He started pulling on his hair again. Poor guy was so frustrated I had to stop myself from bursting out into laughter. I knew exactly what point he was trying to make, but I wasn't going to let him dictate when and where and how I lost my virginity. My whole life I'd been the poster child for following every rule I could but this time I wanted to do things my way. Not be so uptight and safe. I didn't know if I would ever feel this way again with anyone else but I knew that I needed to feel this way for my first time. I wanted to be closer to D-Waite than to any living human being and I wanted a damn orgasm. Some of my girlfriends at school who had already done it said to make sure you got an orgasm first or else the guy gets his and it's all over. Something told me that D-Waite wasn't one of those guys, that he would leave me satisfied, and that's why I wanted to do this.

"Fuck! You killing me, girl." He sighed.

"Good. Then you should just do what I say."

"You know there is no going back?"

"I wouldn't want to," I said, then climbed on top of him and planted a long, slow, deep kiss on him just to remind him that I really was a grown-up. It was halfway until my eighteenth birthday and I intended to start celebrating early. I smiled at myself. I had never felt this confidant and grown-up. I kissed him again. "Now are you going to take my virginity or should I offer it to someone else?" I teased him.

He took my face in his hands and looked me in the eyes. "Don't even joke about that. You are mine."

"And you are mine," I responded, feeling an intensity like nothing I'd ever felt before in my life. I wanted this to last forever.

"If you want to stop just say it. Okay?" He had gotten all intense on me but I liked it. No one made me feel as loved as he did at that moment.

"You sure do talk a lot." I started kissing on his earlobe. Reading that Fifty Shades of Grey *book and* Cosmo *magazine came in handy. Of course I wasn't talking about the dark stuff but all that sex made me anxious to do it.*

My whole body felt on fire just thinking about the way he had licked the insides of my thighs, traveling up until his face was in my pussy. I couldn't describe the pleasure I had experienced as he took me to orgasm. Unless you've had one it's hard to explain how deeply satisfying and powerful it is to let go that completely. It's like you're fighting off this huge avalanche and at the last minute you stop and let it take you. My body was in spasms for what felt like forever.

I had been having these mini shocks down between my legs all day. Just thinking about the things D-Waite did to my body brought me close to orgasm. I'd been so distracted thinking about his hard, thick penis that when Mrs. Broady called on me in French class I had no idea what she was talking about. My classmates all giggled at me because I was known for being a teacher pleaser and always having the answer. Funny that I wasn't even embarrassed. All I wanted was to be back in that bed with D-Waite. By the time the bell rang signaling last class I had reached the end of my rope. I needed him.

I texted D-Waite on my bus ride home, promising him lots of pleasure if he met me at his apartment. He reminded me to be careful and said he'd bring some food. When I exited the B54 I saw that girl Naynay flirting with one of the boys who always harassed me when I got off the bus. I had to walk past them to cross the park, and for a moment I thought of going the long way, but I was too excited to see D-Waite. I put my head down and tried to hurry past, but she noticed and stepped in front of me, blocking me from moving.

"Where you rushing to, bitch?" Naynay spat the words out at me. I folded my arms over my chest and didn't speak.

"So you bad now?" She pushed a pointy, glittered fingernail into my chest. I moved away out of her reach. "You better be keeping away from D-Waite if you know what's good for you."

"Serious? D-Waite's hitting that?" The idiot in the saggy pants came forward, giving me an X-ray look up and down as if imagining me naked. "Damn, Dame gets all the new pussy."

I frowned, scowling at being referred to as my anatomy. "I don't have time for this." I glared at Naynay.

"Oh you bad now? Ready to kick my ass?" She high-fived her friend.

"You better leave her alone. You know Dame don't play around. I wouldn't go messing with his piece."

"She ain't messing with him. Are you?" She stepped in my face, her beady eyes studying me.

"It ain't none of your business." The words slid out before I could stop them.

"Sounds like a yes to me." He laughed.

"Bitch, Im'a tell Mika and she's gonna kick your little schoolgirl ass back to wherever you come from. We told you not to fuck with her man."

"He ain't her man. He's mine." I didn't know what got into me, but hearing her call D-Waite Mika's man made me territorial. I wasn't about to let her think he was her personal property. No. He was my man.

"Whoa! Guess schoolgirl told you." He whooped loudly, dancing around Naynay like a fool. She narrowed her eyes, staring at me.

"Guess she's gonna get a chance to tell Mika to her face." She broke out into the biggest, nastiest smile. My stomach suddenly felt as if someone had kicked me. Mika and another one of her girls, the short one, were coming toward us. I didn't wait to see what was gonna happen. I just took off down the block into the entrance of the park.

I heard footsteps closing in behind me. I pulled out my phone and dialed. "I'm in the park. They're coming after me!" I shouted as I attempted the sixty-yard dash; but with the heaviness of my backpack weighing me down I couldn't move as fast as I needed.

Someone grabbed me by the backpack and yanked me back, flinging me to the ground. I threw my hands over my face as feet started kicking and slamming into me. I tried to get up but arms kept shoving me back down to the ground.

"Get off her!" I heard D-Waite shout at my perpetrators. Then, his arms were around me, pulling me to my feet and comforting me. "Mika, what the fuck is wrong with you?"

"Me? Your little bitch don't belong around here."

"She belongs with me! And if any of you have a problem with that then you need to take it up with me. Gabby hasn't done anything to you," he raged at them, holding me close.

"Her kind don't belong in out hood," Naynay shouted at him. "Rich little bitch."

"Fuck you know about her kind? Her dad used to run the Cumberland and I don't think he'd appreciate you putting your hands on her."

"Bullshit! I ain't never seen her around here. Who her daddy?" Mika shot him a look like she didn't believe him.

"Big John." He dropped the name like the heavy weight that it was. They all backed up, surprised expressions covering their faces. "Yeah, and like I said I don't think he'd appreciate you all fucking with his daughter."

"Whatever!" Mika shot out, but something in her voice had changed. And she stared at me for a long time. It felt weird to have someone study me the way she did. I couldn't figure out what she was thinking and whether it was fear, respect, or something else, but before I could think too long, D-Waite let me go and moved in front of her.

"You and me, Mika? We done!"

"Fuck you then, and don't come begging for none of my good pussy when that uptight schoolgirl can't do nothing for you." Mika made a motion and her two girls followed her out of the park.

"How you feel?" He brushed off the leaves and dirt off my clothes.

"Why did you tell them about my father?" I hissed at him. I could barely admit it to myself and now everybody was about to know the truth about my paternity. Shit!

"I didn't have a choice. I'm not always around so I can't protect you; but your father's name, that's something else. Nobody is gonna try to fuck with you 'cause they are too scared of how long his reach is, even from inside prison. They may lock him up but they can't take away the power he has in these streets."

I wanted to be mad but I knew he had a point. There was something surreal about having a father who I'd never met protect me from a distance. D-Waite and I waited until they were gone to head back to his place.

11

By the time I got to my aunt's house later on all of the lights were off. A few minutes after I undressed and got into bed my door opened. I grabbed hold of the knife I had placed under my pillow before I came into my room. If that motherfucker was gonna try to bother me he was gonna be in for a shock. I'd taken all of the bullshit I could for one day and nobody was gonna put me in victim mode again. *Ever!* I promised myself.

"Gabby." My aunt's voice was a whisper as she came toward me.

I took my hand off the knife as she sat down next to me. "What?"

"Are you okay?" She sounded worried.

"Yeah, I'm good."

"I heard some kids outside talking about you. Did you tell them that Big John was your father?"

"It slipped out by accident," I lied, not wanting to bring up D-Waite's involvement in outing my paternity.

"You sure you want people to know? What if he finds out?"

"I don't know. Is it true?"

"Of course it's true. Your mother spent her entire life protecting you from him and the life he choose."

"Well, my mother isn't here anymore. I'm not saying that I want to get to know him, but suddenly I have this one living parent. That means I'm not alone."

"You're not alone. You have me." She leaned in and kissed me on the cheek. "And you have Preston," she added, but I didn't respond. "You like him don't you?"

"Auntie, maybe you're moving too fast. How well do you know him?"

"I know him well enough to be sure I ain't gonna ever do any better."

"That's not true. You have the world's best heart. Any man would be lucky to have you," I insisted.

"Honey, you'll see when you're older that things don't always work out the way you dream. But, if you're lucky enough to get a second chance at love, you take it, and that's what I'm doing."

"Well why does he have to move in?"

"Because it would help us with the bills. Starting next week we'll get your social security but things are tight for us."

"Can't we make it the next six months? Then I will be gone and the two of you can move in and not have to worry about me in your space."

"I like having you around and I know Preston does too. But he's worried that you don't like him."

"He's here all the time," I whined.

"'Cause I want him here. He never had a family so he wants us to be his family. Isn't that sweet?"

"I just want it to be the two of us." I couldn't help the begging but I was desperate.

"Your mother ruined you by never dating or having men around."

"She was protecting me. I didn't understand that then but I do now."

"What you tryin'a say, Gabby?" Her voice raised and I could hear the fear. She was afraid I would destroy her fantasy.

"Nothing. Do what you want. It's not like I get a vote." I resigned myself.

"No, you don't."

"Well can I at least get that lock on door? I just need my privacy."

"Sure!" Her voice softened. "You all right, Gabby? I was seventeen once so I remember what it's like to be out there dating guys and not thinking."

"I'm thinking."

"No, you not. You start liking a boy at your age, all thinking goes flying the fuck out the window. Shit, truth is that don't never change with age. You being careful?"

"Yes, I'm being careful."

"Using protection?"

"Ugh!" I groaned. "Are we really having this conversation? Because it's embarrassing." I wanted to crawl underneath the bed.

"Ain't nobody ever had this talk with me so everything I learned was from some horny-ass boy tryin'a get in my pants."

"I had the birds-and-bees talk a long time ago." I reminded her of my age.

"It's one thing to have it and another to need it."

"I got it all covered. Thank you." We both laughed. She stood up to leave.

"You know what you gonna do about your father?"

"No," I admitted.

"'Cause now that folks know it may not be too long before he does too. The people around here ain't known for their ability to keep shit to themselves."

"You think he's gonna find out?"

"I can bet he will."

"You know him. What do you think he's gonna do? Do you think he'll even care that I'm his daughter? I mean how many kids does he have? Do you know? A guy like that must have a gang of baby mamas."

"No. As far as I know he never had kids. Well, none that he knows about. Now get some sleep and the next time you decide not to come home you need to call me. You're about to be eighteen, which makes you an adult, so don't make me worry about you."

After she left I couldn't stop thinking about my father. What if I really was his only child and what if he wanted to be in my life? Or what if he rejected me? And did I really want to get to know a man who had done the things he must have done to land in prison for twenty-five years to life? But wasn't my boyfriend doing the same things that my father had done? What a hypocrite I was being.

I spent the next hour or so playing scenarios in my head. *Maybe I should go visit my father. Yeah, why wouldn't I?* I knew that it was a real risk going to see him but I had to at least try to put some closure on this new dad thing. And maybe seeing him would help me to understand what my mother felt about him. My whole life she'd never dated, never even had any male friends around me. She said it was for my protection but I always knew differently. She wasn't willing to risk her heart again. Clearly she had done that at one point with my father. I had to meet the man who had turned my mother away from men. He had obviously broken her heart and, yet, she must have loved him, or why else would she have kept his child? And that's when it hit me. My mother didn't just keep me away from Big John because of his lifestyle. She kept me away because she loved him and somehow he had really hurt her. I picked up my phone and made a call.

"Hey." I couldn't help smiling knowing that he was on the other end of the line.

"Hey, schoolgirl," he joked.

"So if I wanted to visit my father how would I do it?" I assumed D-Waite knew all the ins and outs of the criminal justice system. He admitted that he had done some time, "a bid," in juvie.

He said he'd call me right back. Five minutes later D-Waite told me that my father was in Elmira Penitentiary, a place they called "the Hill." He said that if I had ID he could arrange for me to visit on Saturday as long as Big John agreed to see me. Of course I wouldn't know that until I got there. If I decided to go. I fell asleep, confused about what to do.

It was dark outside when I woke up. Something was wrong. I was certain of that but I wasn't immediately sure what it was. Then I felt a hand sweep over my ass. The covers were off me. I jumped damn near across the room.

"Now I wouldn't do anything stupid if I were you," Preston warned me.

"Get out!" I screamed.

"Shhhh! You wanna wake your aunt? Have me tell her that you've been propositioning me? Begging me to teach you everything I know," he threatened.

"You touch me and you won't have to worry about my aunt." I tried to dive under the pillow for the blade but he stood in my way.

"Why you little bitch. I was willing to take care of you and your aunt. You think that young punk can teach you anything? He don't know shit!" He grabbed my breasts and began to squeeze them roughly. I kicked and pushed until his hands released me. But I could tell that he wasn't done.

"Get out!" I screamed. "Oooout!"

My aunt flung open the door and flicked on the lights. Preston stood there, naked except for his boxers.

"I thought I heard something," he lied.

My aunt looked from me, my arms folded around my chest. "What the hell you doing in here with my niece?' she confronted him.

"You accusing me of something?"

"Gabby, what happened?" she demanded.

"I don't have to stay and listen to her lies." Preston shot out of the room.

Aunt Kim flew after him. "I can't believe you would try anything with Gabby. She's a child," she yelled at him.

"Well she looks like a grown-ass woman," he yelled at Kim.

"You asshole. How dare you?" She raised her voice at him.

"She's the reason I came around so much," he snarled, using the cruelest tone. "You don't think it was you," he tormented her. "Who could really want you?"

I grabbed my bathrobe and ran into the front room. He had almost finished dressing. "Get out and stay away from my aunt. She deserves better than your ass." I opened the front door. "Out," I demanded. My aunt wasn't looking at us. She was fidgeting, pacing around like a caged animal. "And leave the keys," I reminded him. Preston slammed the keys onto the floor and left. I went toward my aunt.

"I'm sorry, Auntie. I should have said something but you were happy and I thought that if I could avoid him . . ." My voice trailed off.

"He been bothering you? How long?"

"A week."

"I'm so sorry, Gabby."

"It's not your fault. He was an asshole."

"It's like I'm a magnet for the worst men," she cried. My aunt crumpled, the air draining right out of her.

"It's gonna be all right. You really do deserve better." I tried to comfort her.

"Did he really try to hit on you? Could he have been kidding?" she pleaded, as if she wanted me—no, needed me—to lie, but I couldn't. I wouldn't.

12

On Saturday morning I woke up at 3:00 A.M.
to get to the bus stop in downtown Brooklyn to
take the bus to Elmira. I told my aunt that I was
going and that I would spend the night with a
friend from school who lived closer. Of course
that friend was D-Waite. It's not that I had to
lie about being with my boyfriend but she had
been depressed since Preston left, and I didn't
want to shove my happy love life in her face.
D-Waite arranged for a cab to pick me up. He
also insisted on giving me a hundred dollars for
the trip even though I told him I had it covered.

I got to the bus stop and stood in line with a lot
of single women and families. There were only
a couple of women on the bus when I boarded.
I grabbed a seat next to a window and went to
sleep, which wasn't hard because D-Waite and I
had spent most of the night not sleeping. I woke
just as the bus driver stopped outside the prison.

I followed the other passengers, who knew the routine.

"You going to visit your man?" an older woman with kind eyes asked me.

"No. My father," I said. Strange that a week ago I'd never said the word out loud and here it was rolling off my tongue.

"Must be really looking forward to seeing him. How long since you done seen him?" she wanted to know.

"I've never met him," I admitted, and suddenly felt embarrassed and stupid for getting on this bus and traveling hours to visit a man who may have wanted nothing to do with me.

"Well aren't you brave. Pretty thing like you. Any man would be proud to have a daughter like you." I smiled in response because I didn't know what to say. "If he refuses to see you then just fuck him. It'll be his loss."

Eventually a door opened and we were led into a screening room where we had to give our identification and say who we had come to visit. The gruff corrections officer stared down at my ID and scowled at me.

"A person under the age of eighteen needs to be accompanied by an adult."

"But I'm going to be eighteen soon," I pleaded.

"Well you can come back then," she barked at me.

The lady I met in line stepped up to the desk.
"She ain't got to be eighteen if she visiting her
daddy."

"Why didn't you tell me that the prisoner was
your father? What's his name and ID number?"

"I don't have his ID number but his name is
John Thompson."

The guard did a double take. "Big John
Thompson?"

"Yes, that's him," I answered, relieved that she
knew who I was talking about.

"He know you coming?" Her voice had taken
on a more respectful tone.

"No, ma'am."

"Wait over there." She pointed to another line.

It felt like I waited forever. A woman was
turned away and wound up screaming obsceni-
ties at the officers. They had to threaten to ban
her from visiting again if she didn't behave.
That's when I learned there was only one bus
and it waited outside until visiting hours were
over. I wondered if I would be in her shoes in
a minute. Who knew how many people had
come to visit men they had been told were their
father? I only had my mother's word, and since
she'd lied to me about my father my whole life I
suddenly didn't know if I could even trust it.

"Gabrielle Davenport!" another guard called out. I went over and he led me through a series of heavy, clanging steel doors until I was in what looked like a public school cafeteria. "Wait here!"

He left the room, but there were a few other officers guarding the prisoners. Mostly women and children sat on metal picnic tables visiting inmates all around the room. People kept buying things out of the vending machine against the back wall. Just the sight of food reminded me that I hadn't eaten yet. Even though it was only eight o'clock, I'd already been up for five hours. I glanced all around the room until I saw the door where the inmates were being led through. The door opened and a tall, imposing man with a short haircut and a manicured beard entered. His eyes took in the entire scope of the room, eventually coming to rest on me. With a few strides he stood across from me.

"Sit." It sounded like a command and I knew to follow it. This wasn't a man used to his orders being disobeyed. He studied me before saying anything more. Finally he spoke.

"So she kept you." His words shocked me.

"You knew about me?"

"I knew that your mother was pregnant. I didn't know that she hadn't gone through with the abortion."

"Abortion! Sorry I wasted your time." I started to stand up but he grabbed my hand.

"That was her idea. I wanted her to keep our baby."

"You did?" I relaxed down in my seat.

"Yes. I did, but your mother hated my life. She didn't want you anywhere near it. That's why she lied, because she knew if she told me that I had a child I would have never abandoned her or you."

"But how do you even know that I'm your daughter? Maybe I belong to some other man."

He burst out laughing. "Did you know your mother? She wasn't like that. Besides you look just like my mother did at your age."

"I do?"

"Yes. So your mother must have told you about me?"

"No, she never said anything. My Aunt Kim told me a few days ago."

"And Evelyn?" The look on my face must have told him everything he needed to know. "What happened?" He didn't hide the hurt in his eyes.

"Cancer. She died three weeks ago." I couldn't believe it was that recent. It seemed so long ago with everything that had happened.

"Who's taking care of you? You must be, what, sixteen? No, you're seventeen."

"And a half. I live with my Aunt Kim at Cumberland housing projects."

"Your mother would not have wanted that. She didn't want you near that place."

"I'm graduating in May and then I'm off to college. It's not that long."

"College? You're going to college?" He started grinning like a proud father. "Where you going?"

"Harvard if I can work it out. My scholarship doesn't cover it all but my dean is helping me look into some grants."

"Harvard? Your mother did a real good job with you. Really good. She must have been proud," he said softly, sounding equally as proud.

"Yeah, she was."

"You need anything? Anything?"

"No, I just wanted to see you. To . . . I don't know. With my mother gone I guess I . . ."

"I'm glad you came."

"Why did you see me? You didn't know. Do you get a lot of visitors claiming to be your children?"

"No, you're the first. I did hear there was some girl in the Cumberland claiming she was my child. It made me nervous because I was really careful. I made a point to be careful not to have no baby mamas. I figured anybody bold enough to lie to me deserved a chance to do it to my face. I never thought I'd actually have a child."

"And now you do," I added.

He leaned in and lowered his voice. "I am your father. You are my child, Gabrielle, and that means that you are under my protection. Is there anyone who needs to be dealt with?" His voice took on a dark, ominous tone.

"No, I'm okay."

"You sure?"

I nodded. For a second I thought about Preston, but then I realized how much it would hurt my aunt and I let it go.

We talked and caught up for the next almost five hours. I learned about his childhood and how he and my mother met and fell in love in ninth grade. He told me about his family, most of his relatives, wound up working for him and many of them ended up behind bars. His mother passed away a couple of years ago and he had been allowed to attend the funeral. I told him about my life before my mother died and about school. The only person I left out was D-Waite. Something told me that he wouldn't be cool with his daughter dating a drug dealer.

"Five minutes!" a guard yelled out, signaling the end of visiting day.

"Gabrielle, I don't want you to take this the wrong way because today has been the highlight of my life. But, I don't ever want you to come back here."

"But—" I started to protest before he interrupted me.

"It's not that I don't care or that I don't want to see you. I do, but not inside these walls. You don't belong inside here. Give me your phone number."

I told him the number with tears stinging my eyes. "Aren't you gonna write it down?" I worried.

"I got it. It's the most important number I know." He brushed away my tears with his hand. "I'm gonna have someone contact you. His name is Bruce. If you ever need me I want you to go through him. He's safe."

"Will I ever see you again?"

"I hope so. I could be out in seven. We'll see."

"Can I write you?"

"Yes, but just know that these people read everything. Be careful what you put down in writing and don't worry about anything. You'll be taken care of."

"But I'm fine."

"I know, but you're also my child." He stood up and I did the same. For a moment neither of us knew how to react. Finally I went to him and threw my arms around him. I realized that this may be the only chance I may ever get to hug my father so I had to take it. A sigh of relief left my lips when he wrapped his arms around me.

"Thompson!" the guard called out in warning, but I noticed that he used a different tone than I'd heard him use for the other inmates. This one was tinged in respect and apology. Big John turned and smiled as he walked out of the visiting room.

In the line for the bus I saw the woman who had spoken to me earlier. "It must have gone good with your father. You look happy."

"Yeah, it did."

"I bet you're glad you took a chance and came to visit him."

"Yes, I am." I grinned. Maybe my life was actually going to be all right.

13

"Yeah, I told him not to be stupid," one of the passengers on the bus shouted into her phone. "Shit, those COs will fuck you up just for looking at them wrong," she continued. "But his ass gotta be a hard rock. Uh-huh, you got that right." She sat directly in front of me, carrying on her conversation like she was sitting alone in her living room. Most of the other passengers were half asleep, drained from the experience of visiting their loved ones behind bars.

"Jesus Christ!" someone snapped, but the woman on the phone didn't hear or she chose to ignore them.

"Bitch, I told you that I told him that. Ain't you listening to nothing I said?" she hollered at the person on the other end of the phone.

"We all listening. You talking so loud we ain't got no choice," a woman responded to her comment.

"Well I was minding my business. Why don't you mind yours?"

"Because you talking so loud you done made it mine. Hell, I can't hear myself think you making so much damn noise."

"Hold on," the woman spoke into the phone.

"It's just rude," another person added.

"Some people don't have no home training. Telling all their business," one of the few men on the bus added. I got nervous, bracing for a full-scale revolt against the woman on the phone.

"I'ma call you when I arrive. These Negros acting all crazy." She hung up to lots more comments and a few cheers. Aside from that incidence the ride home was uneventful.

The entire bus ride back I replayed the visit over and over in my head. It could have just as easily gone the other way with him rejecting me or not believing me, but none of that happened and now I had a father. Growing up I had craved a dad, someone to show me how to ride a bike and protect me from weirdoes.

"Not everybody gets a father. Some people don't even have a mother," my mom would always explain to me when I complained. After a while I stopped saying anything and kept the loss to myself. I didn't want to make her feel bad that she wasn't enough, because the truth was she could never be a father to me. It didn't matter how many times people referred to her as both the mother and the father; I always knew the difference. When I'd see kids with their daddies I used to ache. It got to a point where I would pretend that my friends' fathers were mine, but it wasn't the same and I knew it. But now it appeared that I was one of those people who had a father; only he wouldn't be taking me anywhere or spending quality time together with me.

D-Waite was waiting for me when I got off the bus. The big-ass smile on his face made me so happy. I'd texted him when I left the prison but I didn't expect him to be there.

"Come here." He opened his arms to embrace me. "You must be tired. So tell me everything. Did you see him?"

"Yeah, I did." A smile broke out on my face. "I'm his daughter."

"Really? No blood test? No drama?"

"No. He said that I look exactly like his mother did at my age."

"Guess you're not my favorite little orphan anymore." He kissed me on the lips.

"As long as I'm still your favorite something."

Instead of playing with me he grew serious and nervous, like he was keeping some secret and didn't know how to tell me something. It was the same way my mom acted when she had to tell me she was sick.

"What? You're making me nervous." My stomach started churning.

"Call your aunt." He held my hand. "Do it."

I retrieved my phone and dialed the number. "Hi, Auntie." I was so excited to share my news with her but her voice was shaky.

"Hey, baby," she mumbled.

"You all right?"

"Fine, just tired."

"You don't sound so good. I'm coming home."

"Nah, I'm . . . I won't be here. I'm going out for a walk." She slurred her words as she hurried off the phone.

I stared at D-Waite. "She sounded terrible."

"She's using again," he told me.

"Are you sure? I mean how do you know?"

"One of my boys told me yesterday that she bought from him. I thought I fixed it."

"What did you do?"

"I made sure no one would sell to her. Let's get a cab." We hopped a cab to Cumberland and got to Aunt Kim's in about ten minutes. When we pulled up outside I saw Mika, Naynay, and the rest of their group hanging out on the steps of the next building. She stuck her middle finger up at me as we passed but didn't say anything. D-Waite took my hand and led me inside the building. I was sure that didn't buy me any points with those girls. We entered the apartment, which looked as if someone had tossed it searching for something. My aunt was nowhere to be found.

"Oh my God! What if something happened to her?"

"What did she say?"

"That she was going for a walk."

"Let's go." D-Waite grabbed my hand and we hurried outside. He approached a couple of guys out front.

"Y'all seen her aunt?"

"Kim. She's my height, brown long hair?" I pleaded.

"Crackhead Kimmie?" one of them asked, clearly familiar with her.

"Man, why you gotta go there?" D-Waite chastised the guy.

"Have you seen her?"

"She just went that way." He pointed to the backside of the building.

"She on it?" D-Waite asked.

"If she ain't then she about to be. She had the itch, man."

"Gab, go back inside and wait for me." D-Waite motioned toward the door.

I shook my head, refusing to budge. "I'm going with you." I stood my ground.

"You can't. You shouldn't see this," he warned me.

"Let's go!" I took his hand.

"Shit! Fine, but this was not my idea." He picked up the pace and led me around the back of the building across the street and down a block. As seedy as Cumberland was, this took it down to a much lower level. This was the skid row of Brooklyn. Homeless people were milling around, sleeping right in the middle of the block, drinking, and getting high. This appeared to be a lawless haven for debauchery and criminal activity. A young kid ran up to D-Waite.

"You holding, man? I'm wiped clean."

"Fuck out of here!" D-Waite shouted at him.

"I got customers need some shit," he pleaded.

"I'm clean, man. I can't help you."

The guy started to walk away.

"Wait. Bizzy, you seen a woman people call Crackhead Kimmie?" He glanced apologetically at me.

"Yeah, she went up there."

"Shit!" He slapped his hands over his face.

"What?" I moved his hands from over his eyes.

"You don't need to see what's up in there," he warned me again, but I took his hand and led him in the direction Bizzy had pointed.

The moment we entered the abandoned building the stench of stale vomit, feces, and urine overtook me. I had to cover my mouth to keep from retching my guts out.

"You a'ight?" D-Waite stopped me. "We can kill this whole thing."

"No, let's go." I followed him down a long hallway, and up a rusty steel staircase. Along the way we passed sleeping bodies, shopping carts, and even a dog or two. I tried not to stare at the people as we passed them in order to respect their privacy but it was hard. Some were doing things in public that I wasn't sure should have even been attempted in private. This was the very bottom rung of life and I couldn't believe that my aunt had willingly come in here. D-Waite led me up two flights of stairs and down a hallway to a door.

"This is a shooting gallery. Where the heads go to get blazed up. It's not gonna be pretty." He tapped three times and the door opened. A short guy with dreadlocks opened his mouth wide, revealing a toothless smile.

"Dame. I didn't know you made special deliveries. Set me up?"

"Nah, I'm just looking for someone." He pushed past the guy into the room.

"But if you got some you want to get rid of I'm first. Okay? I'm gon . . . gon . . . gonna be first," he stuttered behind us.

Everywhere I looked junkies were shooting up and nodding off all over the place. There were young, old, every color, people scratching their skin off; a few of the women were half naked, exposing dirty bras and breasts. A beautiful young girl was half naked, hugged up with a flashy pimp who looked old enough to be her grandfather. Just the sight made my skin crawl but I knew I couldn't do anything to help her. We went through a couple of open doors and saw more of the same. We passed a door that was slightly ajar. I thought that I saw something so I stopped. D-Waite followed the direction I was looking and pushed the door open. There was my aunt, her blouse undone as a skinny guy in front of her felt her up.

"But I need it. I just got a little taste today," she begged.

"Now you needy. Reason nobody wants to sell to your ass came from high up."

Kim looked up, shocked to see us enter the room. The guy turned and that's when I saw that his pants were undone. Her hand was is his pants. My aunt's eyes got wide.

"Hey, baby! How you doing?" She moved her hands away from him.

"Aunt Kim, what are you doing in here?" I shouted at her.

"I was just visiting my friend," she tried to cover.

"Dame, man, you got some stuff? I got a few dollars." The guy pulled out a small stack of bills. D-Waite waved his money away.

Suddenly Aunt Kim focused on him. "This your friend, honey? Well I'm her aunt. Can you get my friend some of what he needs?" She was all jumpy and rubbing her arms.

"We have to get out of here." He took on a sterner tone than I was used to hearing.

"But my friend. He needs a little fix. Not a big one. Just a little one. I mean I can give you the money. I got money but nobody will help me. I mean help him." She was acting all manic and crazed.

"Let's get you out of here." He took her arm and led her out.

She grabbed on, clinging to him. "I can be real nice to you," she purred.

"Aunt Kim. This is my boyfriend!" I snapped.

"Yeah, well he a man and a man needs a woman. Don't worry. I ain't trying to keep him or nothing."

D-Waite leaned in, whispering in my ear, "It's the drugs talking."

By the time we got my aunt onto the sidewalk she had propositioned him four more times.

"What now?" I asked as he headed toward Cumberland. Junkies kept begging D-Waite for drugs.

"Back to your place."

A big black SUV pulled alongside us and stopped. It was the same one that had violently taken D-Waite. Aunt Kim broke away and hurried toward the closed doors. The window rolled down.

"Hey, Poppa, how you doing? I don't know what's wrong. I got money and nobody will take it. "

"What?" a deep voice from inside the car barked.

"Yeah, like nobody."

"Dame," the voice shouted.

D-Waite let go of my hand and went over to the car.

"How come one of my favorite customers can't get her hand on what she needs?"

"Yeah, how come?" Kim acted all big and bad, nothing like the aunt I'd gotten to know this last year.

"I don't know," D-Waite said, but I could tell he was lying 'cause his voice sounded terse.

"Fix it," the voice snapped before the windows rolled up and SUV sped off. D-Waite looked worried.

"You can't sell to her," I whispered.

"Hell yes, he can," she shouted, sounding pleased with herself.

"You promised my mother that you would stay clean. That you would take care of me. What happened to that?"

"I tried." Her voice weakened.

"No, when Preston came around you started blowing off your meetings and just did everything for him."

"I did not do everything for him. There were things he wanted me to do that I didn't."

"Like what?" D-Waite asked.

"Nothing. Just nothing. You gonna sell me some rocks or do I have to find Poppa and tell him you disobeyed his order?" She acted tough. D-Waite stared from Kim to me. I had no idea how this was going to resolve but if he gave her any drugs we were through.

14

D-Waite went out to get us some food since I hadn't eaten all day, and who knew how long it had been since my aunt had eaten anything. After my visit to the shooting gallery I couldn't say that I had an appetite. I really wanted to get my aunt to eat something. Maybe if she put some food in her system it would help. Couldn't hurt.

D-Waite told me to make sure that she didn't leave the house. I tried to reason with her and to get her to a meeting or rehab or something before her addiction got any worse. She wouldn't give me her twelve-step sponsor's phone number. I figured that since she had only been using for the past twenty-four hours it might be easier for her to get back on the wagon. It made sense to me that the earlier the intervention the better, but she wasn't having it. Nothing I said or promised could convince her to go with me and get help. Even when I broke down crying, pleading in my mother's name, it got no reaction from her. Getting high was the only thing that mattered.

"He didn't want me," she said, referring to Preston. "What man is gonna want a woman like me?"

"One who is not a pervert!" I reminded her.

"No, any man who likes me is gonna be like him," she whined, falling deeper to the bottom.

"But, Auntie, that's not a reason to throw away all of your hard work."

"It doesn't matter. None of it matters. I'm always going to be alone. People like me don't really get a second chance," she cried out, sounding broken and hopeless.

"Yes, they do. You will. You just have to stay clean and sober; then anything is possible." I repeated all the things I had heard my mother say to her in the months before she died.

"I just need to get high once. Just one last time and then I will go to a meeting and fix this. See, if I had some then I would feel like I don't need it anymore."

"Do you hear how you sound?"

"Poppa told your boyfriend to get me some drugs. Now if he don't then he gonna have to deal with him. You heard what he said."

"He's not going to give you any drugs. You're my aunt and he cares about you."

"He don't give two shits about me," she hollered. "He cares about you and only you. Now you tell that boy if he knows what's good for him then he will get me my fix."

As soon as D-Waite returned with food Kim started badgering him. "You got my stuff?"

"How about you eat a little something?" He tried to calm her down but she was fidgeting and pacing the length of the room. Her eyes had grown big like saucers. After trying everything to convince us to help her get high she relented.

"I'ma go lie down. Maybe I just need some rest." She went into her room and closed the door. D-Waite and I looked at each other. This was entirely new territory for me.

"At least she's gonna rest. That's a good thing right?" I tried to sound hopeful. He stared at the closed bedroom door. His phone started buzzing with texts. After a few message exchanges he looked worried.

"I got to run an errand. Do not let her out of your sight. You can't trust her," he warned as he left.

I went to her room and checked on her. Just like she said she was lying with her eyes closed. I jumped in the shower. I wasn't sure how long I was in there washing off the prison dirt and the shooting gallery dirt but I tried to be quick. When I got out I went to check on my aunt but she was gone.

15

After I phoned D-Waite and told him Kim had left, it was one of the hardest nights of my life. Almost as hard as when my mother died. He told me to stay put in case she came back. I had a horribly sick feeling in the pit of my stomach. Whenever I called either of them I got no answer. I didn't know if I was gonna lose one or both of the most important people in my world.

D's boss had made it clear that he expected Damon to sell drugs to my aunt or to find someone else to do it. I didn't think he would but I couldn't be sure. Finally I couldn't take waiting so I went to find them. It wasn't the safest place but I left the door unlocked in case she tried to get in.

"Look-see, look-see," Naynay shouted at me as I came out the building. A bunch of people were hanging out, smoking marijuana and listening to music. Somebody had hooked an iPhone up to a portable sound system. Even though it was after midnight there were little kids riding bikes and playing too close to the cloud of pot smoke.

"You got something to say?" Mika sneered at me.

"I was just looking for D-Waite," I admitted.

"He tired of your inexperienced pussy already?" Naynay laughed, high-fiving a girl I hadn't seen before.

"How's your daddy?" Mika snapped at me. "Did you have nice little visit?"

"How you know I went to see my father?" I couldn't hide my shock that she knew I had visited my father.

"For me to know and you to figure it out." She rolled her eyes at me. "Don't be surprised if you wind up right there with him."

"Whatever! Any of y'all seen D?" I asked, but they all stared me down and refused to speak like I was an alien or something. I started heading toward the shooting gallery when Taj rolled up on his bike.

"Your man know you out here? Or are you looking for a new man?" he flirted.

"You seen D-Waite?"

"Earlier. Poppa's not happy! He know what's good for him he'll stay missing. He shut it down for Crackhead Kimmie and some of the guys ratted on him. They always tryin'a come up and they don't care how they do it."

"Is he gonna get in trouble?" I was so worried about him.

"He'll probably let him live." The look of fear on my face must have been funny. Taj busted out laughing.

"What?"

"D-Waite gets out of shit. Dude's like a cat. Most of us did real bids and all he ever got was a few months at juvie. So don't worry your pretty little head."

"I just wish he would call me," I admitted.

"I wouldn't be walking these streets alone if I were you. Real-life shit happens out here, especially at night."

My phone beeped with a message. "I gotta go. Thanks." I took off across the park, not thinking. All through the park I kept seeing derelicts, homeless, and people I wouldn't want to see in the light of day.

"Baby, how much?" a couple of drunks shouted out at me as I passed.

"Hey." I felt someone grab hold of my arm. "Get off of me," I screamed out as I wrenched my arm away.

"This is our place at night," a toothless homeless woman smoking on a cigarette snapped.

"This is our goddamn Vegas," another voice yelled out. "What happens in here stays in here!"

Laughter followed me all the way until I reached the street. I glanced around, making sure no one was following me; then I crossed the street and went inside the apartment. The place was empty and I had to wait a few minutes until D arrived. He looked a real hot mess; his face was scratched up and his clothes ripped.

"What happened?" I screamed, imagining the worst.

"I couldn't stop her. She just had to get that fix."

"So you found her? Where is she?"

"You're gonna have to trust me." He grabbed me by the hands and sat me down.

"Tell me!" I screamed, 'cause now I was imagining the worst.

"I found her and she was nodding off under the bridge near the shooting gallery. She was a real mess. But when I picked her up she started fighting me off, clawing, hitting, and ripping my clothes. I had to get her out of there and quick before any of Poppa's boys saw us. They may be my friends but they're all about tryin'a take my spot. So I got her out of there and I took her to a guy I know. Used to be a huge junkie but he got on the wagon and now he helps people like your aunt get better."

"He runs a rehab?"

"You can call it that. It's a different kind of place."

"Different how?" I got all suspicious and pulled away.

"They don't ask questions and they get results. It's a low-bottom place."

"We got to get her out of there and into a real hospital."

"She'd have to be willing to sign herself up, to commit to a program, and even then we'd have to find one."

"But what do you know about this guy? What if he hurts her?"

"He's not going to hurt her. He's the real deal."

"How can you be sure? What do you really know about this guy?" I saw something in his eyes that worried me. "Tell me."

"He's my father."

"Your father?"

"Yes."

"I thought you didn't talk to him."

"I don't. I mean I haven't spoken to my dad in five years. Growing up he was so addicted to that stuff that he did whatever he needed to in order to get it. He would sneak into our apartment and steal the rent money. He stole my Discman. Our television. Anything he could sell quickly. We were almost homeless and that's when I started working for Poppa. I had to support my moms and sister. I was a lookout, then a courier, and then a dealer. Five years ago my dad gets clean. Comes back to the hood and starts this underground program helping get junkies clean. I'm talking the lifelong addicts. He asks me to give up working for Poppa. Wants me to go back to school. Go back to my dreams, but it's too late for me. I'm too angry and too used to being on my own to trust that I can trust him again. He gets my little sister and my moms out of the projects but I won't go. Not much to say to him after that."

"And you went to see him today? For me?"

D-Waite pulled me into his arms. "Girl, nothing I wouldn't do for you. He's gonna take care of her. Said it can take three to six months 'cause she's broken. Then she'll go upstate to a different program, where she'll get a job and a place away from here and start a new life."

"You did that for me?" The tears kept falling down my face. I glanced up to see that he was crying too. "What, baby?"

"He begged me again to leave this place. I told him about you, that you were leaving in a few months to go off to college in Boston."

"You did?"

"Yeah, and he asked me to go with you."

"Will you?"

"I don't know. What will I do?"

"You can start over. We will have a chance."

"You really want me to go?"

"D, I need you. I need you so much." I collapsed into his arms.

"Then I'm going with you. Baby, I'm going with you."

For the rest of the night we talked about our plans and made love, sweet love, as if it were both the first and last time we'd ever touched that way. I fell asleep exactly where I wanted to be: in the arms of the man I loved.

16

I hurried into the building, glancing around to make sure I wasn't being watched. I saw Mika and her girls but I didn't think they noticed me. They were too busy huddled together, whispering about something. Running up the stairs I took them two at a time. I couldn't wait to get back to D-Waite and to start our new life. Just the thought of him joining me in Boston and leaving this place behind made me want to see him. Hopefully I could gather all my stuff and be out in no time. D asked me to move in with him because he didn't want me in Cumberland.

"You don't belong there," he held my face in between his hands. "I want you to be here with me so that I can protect you." My aunt would be in rehab for six months. The first few months I would still be in Brooklyn and I could check on her. I was so glad that we got her away from that life.

Taking my suitcase from the closet I placed it on the bed, opened it, and started throwing clothes inside. I would use my social security money to pay the rent while my aunt was in rehab but I really hoped she wouldn't come back here. I opened my backpack and put my computer inside. I was so busy daydreaming and packing that I didn't hear the knocking. My stomach sunk at first but then I remembered that it could be one of the real friends Kim had made in the building.

"Who is it?" I called out through the door.

"It's Mika," answered the last person I expected. "Look, I know I'm not your favorite person but I just need to talk to you."

"About what?" I shouted through the door.

"Gabby, I want to apologize." She spoke in a softer tone than I had heard her use before. "I swear I won't do anything to hurt you. If you look at me you will see that I'm serious." It was like she was pleading with me.

After a few moments I opened the door. A more subdued Mika stepped into the apartment, carrying a backpack. It occurred to me that I didn't even know that she was in school. I didn't know anything about her. She offered a warm smile.

"I been a real bitch to you."

I nodded, 'cause it wasn't like I could disagree with her.

"See, D-Waite didn't know that I had real feelings for him. He thought it was just a booty call because I never told him. So when I saw you with him I got jealous. 'Cause to me you were this goody-goody stealing my man."

"I didn't know," I swore.

"I know," she agreed. "It was fucked up of me. I didn't know that you had lost your mother. That must have been tough."

"Yeah, it was," I admitted.

"I lost my father when I was younger. He was murdered." Her voice shook at the memory. "So I know what you're going through."

"Thanks. That means a lot to me."

"We orphans have to stick together."

I nodded my head in agreement.

"Hey, can I use your bathroom? I'll be quick."

"Sure. It's down the hall to the left."

"And can I please have some water?"

"'Kay." I felt so much better as I poured Mika a glass of water. Everything in my life felt like it was turning around. Three weeks ago I thought my life was over and now it was like it was just starting.

Mika came into the kitchen. "Thank you. I got to run."

"Don't you want the water?"

"No. Somebody is waiting for me." She rushed out the door.

"Bye," I hollered out behind her as I locked the door and went back to packing. My phone started ringing immediately.

"You can't wait can you?" I joked into the phone.

"Get out of there right now," he screamed at me.

"I'm almost done." I rolled my eyes at his bossiness.

"Was Mika just there?" he asked.

"How did you know?"

"Did she leave your sight?"

"She went to the bathroom but that's all."

"Get out of there now! She set you up! Run!"

I grabbed my purse and ran to the door just as two uniformed cops were about to knock.

"Going somewhere?" One of them laughed. Within five minutes they had found a pound of pot and fifty rocks of crack cocaine stuffed in my backpack.

17

The handcuffs were digging into my skin. They felt like they were cutting off my circulation as I rode in the back of the police car.

"Where are you taking me?" I managed to stop crying and ask the cops.

"You got a one-way ticket to Rikers." He sneered at me.

"But don't I get a phone call?" I pleaded with him.

"Oh, you'll get your phone call and your useless public defender."

"No wonder this country is in so much trouble. You got these derelict kids with no ambition breaking laws and then demanding to be represented as if they were innocent. And it's us taxpayers who foot the bill for their legal representation. Any other country they'd just skip right over this personal rights bullshit. It's killing our country. You get found with a pound and you go straight to jail."

"But it wasn't mine. I don't know where . . . Well, this girl hates me and she set me up."

"Save it for the judge. He's seen your kind coming and going." He laughed and his partner joined in.

I stared out the window, wondering if this would be the last time I would actually see the outside world. We traveled across a bridge. I saw a small island of buildings and jails. The car pulled up outside a large gray building. They helped me out of the car and led me into the gigantic building. After going through a series of buildings I understood that this was like the Door of No Return on Goree Island off the coast of Senegal. During the slave trade all the slaves were led through this door and onto ships that would carry them to faraway lands away from their freedom. I imagined that this was how the slaves must have felt entering a doorway that guaranteed the end of their old life. I saw quite a few people dressed like me in street clothes. Most were being led into the jail. I saw one man with a huge smile who was obviously leaving.

"I'm outtie!" he shouted as he passed me, an officer leading him out.

Finally I arrived at the Rose M. Singer building, where the women were housed. I felt myself shaking as they led me inside the gates and into a large holding area. This was an entirely different experience from the one I had only days earlier visiting my father. I didn't know who I should phone with my one call but I needed to speak to D-Waite.

The cops signed paperwork, all the while talking about me as if I weren't human. As if I weren't there. It hit me that to them I was one more statistic, another poor black girl who had fallen prey to the criminal element because of my greed to get rich quick. I didn't bother to set them straight because, after all, I was the one in handcuffs, caught with an obscene amount of drugs in my backpack. This was the first time that I was glad my mother wasn't alive. After all her hard work to keep me away from crime and drugs and here I was accused of both. I had let her down. Tears kept rolling down my face even though I tried to be strong.

"Don't cry now." One of the correction officers laughed at me. "You did the crime and now you're gonna do the time. I'm sure you'll make a lot of friends. Those dykes like young fresh meat like you."

"Hell, she'll be wed whether she likes it or not within a week," another one added.

"I hope you like the taste of sushi," a female officer added.

They kept at it until a middle-aged female officer entered through an inside door.

"Y'all leave her alone," she chastised the officers. "Follow me." She directed me through a door. "Have you ever been arrested before?"

"No, ma'am," I whispered.

"How did you get here?" she asked, shaking her head before I could answer.

"My boyfriend—" Before I could continue she interrupted.

"Boyfriend? Huh? It's always some guy who gets young girls in trouble. In the meantime he's out there probably already corrupting some new girl to be his drug mule."

"No, it's not like that!" I defended D-Waite.

"It never is." She took my finger and fingerprinted me. "You're gonna be in here for most of your youth while he's out there free, not thinking about you. These guys are worse than pathological. They use woman. I hope you figure that out before it's too late."

"You don't know him."

"In sixteen years working corrections I have never seen a guy stop his girlfriend from taking the fall for him."

"That's not what happened. It's not his fault."

"Did you have anything to do with drugs before you met him?" She stared me straight in the eyes. I had to look away. We finished the rest of her work in silence. She photographed me, did a strip search, and then she gave me a small bar of soap, a scratchy washcloth and towel, and led me to a shower without a curtain or door.

Maybe it was the water or the reality hitting me but I broke down crying, my entire body racked with sobs. I didn't know how long I had been in there until she yelled out, "Hurry up in there. This ain't no country club."

When I got out and dried off she handed me a bra, panties, and a gray jumpsuit that closed with Velcro. It was the standard uniform that all the prisoners wore.

"Come on." She hit the buttons on a keypad and a large steel door opened. She led me down a hall until we reach a heavily barred door. "Lemme give you some advice: keep to yourself and don't let them see you crying. Weakness will work against you."

"Open!" she yelled out and the door swung open to the inside of the jail. We entered on the lower level where female inmates crowded out of their cells, into an open area, where some watched television or hung around.

"Fresh meat!" a voice yelled as I followed the officer. She led me into a tiny cell with a metal bunk bed, a metal toilet, and a sink.

"This is where you will be until your case is heard. It can take up to forty-eight hours since it's a weekend." She pointed to a lower bunk with a folded blanket on top. "I will make sure you don't have a roommate tonight. Take care of yourself," she warned and then she was gone. As soon as she left two inmates crowded around the door. The heavyset dark-skinned one looked like a man.

"What you in for?" she asked and I swore she sounded just like a dude.

"They found drugs in my backpack."

"So you a mule?" the dude asked but it sounded like a statement of fact.

"You broke the first rule of crime. Don't get caught." The short, pretty Latino woman, about twenty, laughed. The heavyset woman swatted her on the ass.

"Bitch, you glad you got caught. In here, you gotta make the right friends. Ones who will have your back," the big one informed me. "They call me Tiny Tina." She grabbed on to my head, rubbing it like I was a puppy or something. "Shit is real and soft." She smiled to herself.

"Um, I just want to rest." I had been holding back more tears and I remembered the officer's warning not to break down.

Tiny Tina shot me an angry stare. "You rejecting my friendship?"

"No. I just . . . I'm really tired."

"Want me to give you a massage?" She smiled easily at me as if we were old friends or lovers.

"No, thank you." I tried not to appear mortified but I was afraid she wasn't fooled.

"No, thank you," the short Latino mimicked me. "Oooh she's all Miss Manners and shit."

I started to apologize, but then I thought about what D-Waite taught me about letting people see fear, how they immediately treated you as a victim ready to be abused.

"Look, I just need to be alone." I grabbed my blanket, rolled it into a pillow, and lay on the bed with it under my head. Inside I was shaking in total fear but I pretended that I wasn't.

"A'ight, bitch, you wanna fuck off my generous offer of friendship. Don't come begging to suck my dick when you understand that this ain't no high school." Tiny Tina sneered down at me, then turned and walked off with her friend.

There was no way I would be able to sleep. Nobody even knew that I was here. They didn't let me make a phone call so I couldn't talk to D-Waite. I closed my eyes imagining it was six hours ago and I was still with him, that I hadn't gone home to get my things and I hadn't let Mika in. But the noises of the inmates screaming and yelling, arguing and laughing kept me awake.

I glanced up at the small window in my cell. It hurt to even consider looking outside. My whole life I had done all the right things, followed rules, and yet I had wound up in the same place as people who had never walked the straight and narrow. One thing I felt certain of was that my life as I knew it was over.

18

"Breakfast!" one of the women yelled out and jarred me awake. I had been up most of the night listening to sounds, people coughing, having nightmares, and other unidentifiable noises. Heavy metal doors clanged as they opened the cells. Women lined up single file as they headed out to breakfast.

"You ain't hungry, chil'?" an older, grandmotherly-type woman stopped in the doorway to my cell.

"No, ma'am," I answered.

"It's hard at first but you'll get your appetite back."

"Keep moving," a gruff corrections officer shouted and she continued moving down the line. Inmates marched past my cell, staring in at me. I felt naked as they made comments, acting as if I weren't even there.

"Doors closing!" an officer called out as the door to my cell slammed shut.

After everyone had gone to breakfast and no more prying eyes were moving past my cell I got up to use the bathroom. The metal toilet sat right there in the open cell. Sitting on the cold metal I broke down in tears again. I wondered how many tears I even had left. I had to accept that nothing and no one could ever get me out of here. I was almost eighteen, which meant that I would be tried as an adult. I missed Maddie and all the stupid inside jokes we had that no one else found funny. And school, a place where I had always excelled and been treated like I was exceptional. In here I wasn't special. I was simply one more brown-skinned criminal. One more good girl gone bad.

"Gabrielle Davenport," an officer called out as the doors to my cell clanged open. Before I could move the same officer who brought me into my cell stood in front of me.

"Come on! What you waiting for?" she snapped. I followed her back through a series of doors. In the same room where she had given me the prison uniform she handed me my clothes and I changed. I didn't dare speak until after we exited the Rose M. Singer building into a car that took us back to the main building.

"Am I going to court?" I asked.

"No. From what I hear you're going home."

"Home?" The word came out like a question because it didn't make any sense to me. She led me into the building.

"I guess I was wrong. He's not letting you take the fall. First time I ever heard of this happening."

"What are you talking about?" I felt like I was in a fog or some other person's movie. I stood at the counter where I had turned in all of my belongings, as the outside door opened and in walked D-Waite being led in by two policemen. Before I could say anything he lifted a finger to his mouth in the hand movement of silence. The officer handed me my belongings. D-Waite mouthed the words "I love you." I said them back to him and just like that he was led inside the jail as I was being ushered out.

On the cab ride back to Brooklyn all I could think about was the man I loved behind bars. My phone rang.

"Hello!" I answered the blocked number hoping it was D-Waite.

"Gabrielle Davenport?"

"Yes?"

"This is Bruce. Mr. John Thompson told you to expect my call?"

"Yes. Um. Can I call you back?"

"This will be quick. Is anyone listening to you?"

"I'm in a cab."

"Then listen. There is a bank account set up for you from your father's legitimate enterprises. He purchased a building for you at 68 South Portland. Do you understand?"

It was D's apartment building. "Yes." He really did know everything that went on in the outside world.

"All of your things have already been deposited there. You will have adequate money in your account to handle all of your needs in college, including a car and whatever else you need. I will set up an account for your friend so that he will be able to buy anything he needs while incarcerated, and also a phone account so that he can make calls. He's looking at twelve months to two years. Your father would prefer you not visit jail again. Ever. Do you understand?"

"Yes."

"Is that agreeable to you?"

"Yes."

"You have the keys to the apartment?"

"Yes."

"Great. I will have your aunt's apartment packed up and placed in storage. As soon as she is doing better your father will make sure that she is settled somewhere nice."

"Okay. Can I ask you one thing?"

"Sure."

"What happened? Why did Mika set me up?"

"She blamed your father for her father's death. It was her way of getting back at him. But don't worry. She's being handled."

I shuddered, wondering what price she was going to pay for hurting me.

"Oh." I was kind of relieved. It made sense that she didn't do it because of some guy, although D was a hell of a guy.

"Miss Davenport, Big John has a long reach, so whatever you need, if you're ever in trouble, he'll know before you do. And he'll be there to help. Enjoy Harvard." And the phone went dead.

I made the next call. "Hello?" Maddie picked up on the phone on the first ring.

"Gabby, where the heck you been? I haven't spoken to you all weekend."

"I've been crazy but I'll see you tomorrow."

"Wanna come over after school and do your homework?"

"That sounds great," I replied. As I hung up the phone, tears streamed down my face. I had never felt so loved and so alone at the same time. All I wanted was to get home to our place and put on one of D's T-shirts. *It may be awhile before I can see him again but I will wait.* He was worth waiting for.

Friendly Fire

by

Natalie Weber

1

LaRhonda, Keisha, and Shawna

"Damn, bitch, you drunk already? That was only a wine cooler." LaRhonda nudged Keisha next to her.

In a tight circle they sat on milk crates left by the hustlers of the building. Although the stench of piss permeated their nostrils, they ignored it like any other teen living in the projects of East New York, Brooklyn. Keisha, Shawna, and LaRhonda lived in the same building for most of their lives. It was Shawna's birthday and they were celebrating. LaRhonda got the drinks and the smoke from her cousin, Daryl. LaRhonda and Keisha swore they were finally going to get their girl drunk and high on her seventeenth birthday.

Shawna never associated herself with anything bad unless she was proof positive that her parents wouldn't find out. Six months away from early graduation and starting her internship with Lifers Music, one of the newest and hottest labels in the industry, she was what every mom from the hood wanted for their daughter—a way out without getting pregnant by some deadbeat, go-nowhere hustler in the hood.

Everyone who knew Shawna knew her parents, Raymond and Gloria Vasquez. All the local dudes who hung out in front the building purposely stayed far away. There was an understanding between her father and those hustlers hanging in front of the building: if they didn't want any trouble then they wouldn't dare approach his daughter unless they were saving her life. Her mother, on the other hand, wasn't so smooth with her tolerance; her numerous rants of Jesus and the Mother of God kept them at a distance in Shawna's presence.

"It's yo' birthday . . . We gonna party like it's ya motherfuckin' birthday!" LaRhonda and Keisha belted out, singing along with the music from a passing car.

"Y'all so damn stupid. I'm not drunk and y'all ain't getting me drunk either 'cause my father gonna kick my ass. Especially yours, LaRhonda, 'cause you supposed to be taking me to Applebee's and a movie."

"Keisha, can you roll the weed? I don't wanna mess my nails up." LaRhonda fanned her fingers out in front of her face, showing her newly airbrushed acrylic tips at their best.

"Now you know you ain't even supposed to be drinkin' and smokin' anyway. Ain't you knocked up again?" Keisha asked, pointing to her bulging stomach.

"Why don't you mind yo' motherfuckin' business, a'ight?" LaRhonda threw the weed at Keisha. "Here."

"LaRhonda, are you pregnant again?" Shawna asked, surprised.

"That's what I'm sayin', yo' fuckin' ass can't keep shit to yo'self." LaRhonda spat out, pointing her finger in Keisha's face.

"Why y'all keepin' shit from me all of a sudden? Is that what we doin' now?" Shawna's liquid courage started to spill secrets. "You know what? I ain't tellin' y'all nothin' no more. That's why yo' ass gonna get get yo'self killed when Eric find out that ain't his baby in yo' belly!" Shawna let out a burp.

"You fuckin' bitch!" Keisha shouted at LaRhonda.

"Yeah, she ain't tell you that one huh, Keisha? Don't feel good do it?" Shawna reached into the black plastic bag next to the crate and pulled out another wine cooler. Shawna stared at Keisha. "Don't act like you all innocent, too, *mami*. You know what I'm talkin' 'bout . . ." She blew a kiss to Keisha and giggled.

Keisha jumped from the crate and into Shawna's face, almost causing her to spill the wine cooler all over herself. "Stop runnin' yo' fuckin' mouth, Shawna. I ain't gonna feel bad givin' you a black eye for yo' motherfuckin' birthday!"

LaRhonda quickly stood up and tried to get in between the two. "Yo, Keisha, chill! What the fuck is wrong wit' you?"

"Oh, so you just gonna start beatin' on people now? I wish you would—"

"Shawna don't, 'cause yo' ass gonna get thrown off this fuckin' roof. Keisha, just calm the fuck down. She ain't mean nothin'. It's the three bottles she guzzled down in the fifteen minutes we been up here. Just roll up some weed and chill the fuck out. I don't know what she talkin' 'bout so ain't no need to get all fuckin' feisty. It's her fuckin' birthday; let's try to enjoy ourselves. Can we get back to gettin' fucked up and talkin' shit?" LaRhonda waited for Keisha to sit back down before she did the same. "I got way more issues to deal wit' than y'all bickering fools. Keisha, you ain't spark up yet. I need a pull right about fuckin' now."

Keisha sat there for a moment, inhaling the moment. She pulled out some weed and another Dutch Master, then proceeded to roll the blunt. They sat in silence with looks of resentment on their faces.

"I'm sorry. I shouldn't have said nothin'," Shawna said almost in a whisper.

"Now what you gonna do 'bout yo' little situation?" Keisha passed LaRhonda the blunt.

"You better think of something real fast 'cause Eric tried to ask me the other day when I was taking out the garbage," Shawna said.

"Damn, Shawna, when was you gonna tell me that?" LaRhonda asked.

"Ain't nothin' to tell you 'cause my father came out before he finished his question. The only thing he got out was your name and 'is.'" Shawna started laughing hysterically.

"I'm happy you find that so funny, Shawna," LaRhonda shot her a look to kill.

"So who's baby is it?" Keisha asked.

"Why you all in my business?" LaRhonda turned her face, avoiding eye contact with any of them.

"By that question alone I know who. Why in the world would you fuck wit' that nigga again? He ain't beat yo' ass enough the last time you saw him?" Keisha questioned with anger in her voice.

Shawna could see it was getting to Keisha so it was her turn to calm the waters before it got out of hand. "Okay, Keisha, just relax; here, take the blunt. She love that man and she don't care. No matter what we say she ain't gonna ever stop lovin' him."

"That nigga ain't no fuckin' man. He a fuckin' scrub; nah, he the fuckin' turd that comes out my ass every fuckin' mornin'. I'm tellin' you, Ronnie, if I gotta come save yo' ass again from him I'ma kill him." Keisha stood up and lit a cigarette, then walked to the edge overlooking the park in the projects. "Yo, Ronnie, Eric know where you at?

"Why you . . . askin'?" LaRhonda asked with hesitation in her voice.

Shawna and LaRhonda quickly stood up and walked over to Keisha.

"Ain't that his boys over there?" Keisha questioned.

"Fuck!" LaRhonda started to panic.

They heard the door to the roof bang against the wall. They all jumped.

"Damn, y'all plottin' a hit or somethin'? Why y'all jumpin'? You expectin' somebody else?" Vincent stood six foot three, with milk chocolate—colored skin and curly brown hair. He was a brick house; muscles toned and weighing over

250 pounds made him an intimidating figure in the hood.

"Oh shit, Vinnie, what you doin' here?" LaRhonda asked, walking toward him with all smiles.

Vincent laughed. "What the fuck you mean? I'm here to see my baby." He pulled her closer to him and planted a kiss on her lips and gripped her round ass.

LaRhonda quickly thought about what she was supposed to do two days ago. *Fuck, I hope no shit pop off.* "I thought we was gonna see each other tomorrow."

"C'mon now, you know I can't stay away from you . . ." Vincent looked at LaRhonda, confused.

LaRhonda's eyes kept darting away as she tried to loosen his arms around her.

He grabbed her by her arms and squeezed, then whispered into her ear, "You ain't tell yo' punk-ass boyfriend I'm back yet, did ya?"

"Vinnie, I . . ." LaRhonda's voice started to tremble.

Shawna and Keisha looked at each other, then at the empty bottles next to the crate on the floor. They could see LaRhonda's uneasiness. Keisha walked closer to the crate.

"Congrats, Vin. I heard you gonna be a daddy again," Shawna quickly belted out before Keisha could pick up the bottle and throw it in his direction. Moving quickly toward Keisha, she pulled her away from the crate, showing her pearly whites and announcing the newsflash to Vincent, hoping to delay the slap her best friend was about to get.

LaRhonda turned toward Shawna with big eyes and mouthing the words, "Fuckin' bitch."

"What? When was you gonna tell me?" Vincent asked, releasing his tight grip on LaRhonda's arms.

"I'm not sure . . . I was gonna go to the free clinic in the mornin'. I wasn't gonna say nothin' 'til I knew fo' sure." LaRhonda stepped back a bit from Vincent.

"Well, if you is then let me handle that nigga Eric. 'Cause ain't no way he gonna think that's his kid."

"Okay, we all happy for you, aaagain. Now, can you leave so we can get back to celebratin' our girl's birthday?" Keisha shouted out, annoyed at his macho shit.

"Keisha . . ." LaRhonda's voice was stern, eyeing Keisha with I'ma-slap-the-shit-out-you look.

Keisha walked away like a child scorned. Shawna followed suit, not wanting to get into any trouble in her condition.

"Let her say what she want. Like I told you, it was gonna be different. I can't be out in these streets. I . . . We got Diamond to think 'bout. I got this one shit I gotta do and then we straight. We can go down South." His tone and words were sincere; his voice was calm and his eyes were different.

Days before LaRhonda didn't see this side of him. She wouldn't tell her besties that he slapped her again.

"Where the fuck is all this comin' from? Since when you wanna leave here?" She put her hand on her hip and stepped all the way back, staring at him up and down. Even with his sincere words, in the pit of her stomach she felt it; *he's being sneaky*.

Keisha and Shawna looked out over the edge to see who was gathering in the park. They saw Eric walking toward the building when he looked up at them. "Oh shit, I hope this don't turn out bad," Keisha whispered to Shawna.

"We gotta tell her he comin' up here," Shawna said, looking toward LaRhonda, trying to get her attention. She didn't want to interrupt their special moment, but she knew warning her would be better than nothing.

"Ronnie, come here. Shawna's mom is callin' my phone. You gotta answer it. Hurry up."

Keisha made up anything that would make her move.

"Are you serious?" LaRhonda walked over with an attitude. "Vinnie, gimme a sec." She took the quick steps toward her girls. "I didn't hear—"

"Eric is on his—" Shawna pulled her close and tried to talk fast, but didn't get the words out quick enough before they all heard the roof door slam against the wall.

"Wow . . ." Eric rubbed his chin and chuckled a bit when he saw Vincent. "You was havin' a party and didn't invite me . . . That's all good." Eric looked over to Vincent. "We can play nice. I know how to share." He blew a kiss toward LaRhonda. Eric only stood five ten, 150 pounds at the most, with almond-colored skin. His hair always cut close to his scalp. Eric's looks weren't the best, but his eleven-inch dick made up for it every time.

Vincent took a baby step before hearing LaRhonda's voice stopping him from just slamming Eric's body against the rooftop floor or even worse. "Nigga, I should slap the shit outta you." Vincent stepped closer toward Eric, leaving the only opportunity for him to make a move.

Eric showed his Glock 9 tucked into his waistband. "Nigga, I ain't stupid. You think I'ma be out here slippin'?"

"Yo, Eric . . ." LaRhonda tried to get his attention.

"She's prego wit' my seed, nigga. What you got to say 'bout that?" Vincent folded his huge arms across his chest.

"Vinnie . . . Don't—"

"Don't what? This nigga need to back the fuck up like the real bitch he is. What's the problem?" Vincent watched Eric's hands real close. He knew he could cut the distance between them quickly and probably knock his lightweight ass before he could let off one shot.

"Oh my God! Oh my God!" Shawna shouted in fear. After years of sneaking around her parents she just knew this was going to disappoint them to the extreme. She heard the stories and knew this wasn't going to end good. Her breathing started to shorten. Spit started to build in her mouth; she bent her head over trying not to vomit. The fear of disappointment to her parents was more her concern than the gun he just showed. "I gotta get outta here. Ronnie, you gotta take me home, now!"

"I knew you was fuckin' wit' this motherfucker again. I thought you ain't like gettin' smacked around. Let me ask you this then, is it his baby?" Eric looked at LaRhonda.

There she stood with her head down and fiddling with her nails as if she didn't hear the question posed to her. She didn't want it to end like this. Eric was always nice to her and never even raised his voice to her even if she was the one yelling.

"She don't need to answer that." Vincent cocked his head to the side and inched a little closer.

Eric took his hand off his gun and bent over with uncontrollable laughter. "Look . . ." He placed his hand on his stomach, trying to get back to the seriousness of the current situation. "Whew, I'm sorry, my nigga, but you tryin' to tell me even if that my child I don't got nothin' to do with that. All I'm sayin' that bitch pussy ain't worth two cents to me, but I wanna know if that's my child or not. Serious talk my nigga, I'm comin' to you on some man shit. You feel me? 'Cause at the end of the day if you was in my position you would want the same respect."

Vincent wanted to knock his jaw out of place because it didn't matter if the baby was his or not. He was going to be her man regardless. Stepping closer to LaRhonda Vincent asked her, "And what you got to say?"

The sounds coming from Shawna throwing up made everyone stop for a moment.

"Ronnie, we gotta get her out of here. She fucked up."

Hoping Keisha's voice of concern was enough to settle this for now and get Eric's sudden act of courage to die down, LaRhonda looked at both men and shook her head. "Listen I don't even know if I am prego. So y'all niggas arguing over nothin'. Look I gotta get my friend home before shit get real serious." She was mad and those words hit them both with a sting. "Y'all really know how to fuck up somebody's night." LaRhonda walked over to Keisha and helped Shawna to the door.

Eric stepped in front of LaRhonda when she was near the door. "Tell me whose is it. You fuckin' know how long you been fuckin' both of us."

"Yo, son, you need to back the fuck up before I show you how to use that toy," Vincent intervened not liking the small space between them.

"Move, Eric," Keisha shouted, vexed that she would probably have to cancel her plans for later to deal with this bullshit. She couldn't understand what LaRhonda did to these niggas. Her looks weren't Halle Berry and her body definitely wasn't an appeasing full-figured hourglass. "Eric, just fuckin' leave. It's finished. It's done. She chose him. Get over it. Now move so we can get the fuck outta here before—" Keisha held her tongue.

LaRhonda stared at Eric, hoping he would just turn around and leave.

Eric wasn't scared of Vincent's size; it was his five-year bid upstate. He heard stories about niggas like him; niggas with his size was being fucked on the regular. Putting his hand on LaRhonda's stomach he asked her the question again, "Is it mine?"

Vincent's hand reached for Eric's throat. The quick movements made Keisha pull Shawna to one side, separating them from LaRhonda. Eric ducked and Vincent stumbled a bit. Eric jumped back and reached for his gun, pulling it from his waist. Vincent's heart began to beat faster as he secured his eleven-inch Tims to the rooftop. As he turned around to face Eric, his eyes met the Glock up close and personal. He eased back slowly, not wanting to make any sudden moves because LaRhonda was near.

LaRhonda called out to Eric, pleading for him to just leave it alone until she had her doctor's appointment to confirm that she even was pregnant. It was evident that this wasn't going to end reasonably. She stepped in front of the gun. "Eric, you ain't doin' nothin'. That is the father of my firstborn and you are not gonna take him away just 'cause I'm fuckin' him. If you gonna shoot him then make sure you shoot me and Diamond 'cause he the one who been feedin' us. Let's be real 'bout that shit. The only reason I started fuckin' wit' him again was 'cause yo' ass was too busy runnin' wit' yo' dime-bag hustlers. Nigga, don't you see shit need to be better, not the same ol' same ol'? Get the fuck outta here wit' this I-got-a-big-gun-and-I-need-to-show-it-off complex. It's fuckin' lame."

Eric's ego was crushed. He lowered the gun, not posing any threat, but still held it in his hand. He was calm when he asked, "You willing to let this nigga use yo' ass as a punchin' bag anytime he feel like it?" He waited for a moment, then looked to Vincent over LaRhonda's shoulder; she took too long to answer. "You know what, my nigga, you could have this bitch. She like gettin' hit, y'all belong together!" Eric put his gun back into in waist and exited the rooftop.

With a sigh of relief, LaRhonda looked to Vincent. "If you serious then you do whatever you got to do to make it right, 'cause you know how me and Diamond livin'." She faced Keisha and Shawna. "C'mon let's fuckin' go."

Stunned at LaRhonda's unexpected request Keisha almost let out an "Amen." Keisha grabbed Shawna's arm and helped her to the door.

LaRhonda aggressively grabbed Shawna's other arm and exited the rooftop, leaving Vincent standing there. She began to rant as they slowly descended the stairs, "What the fuck is wrong wit' ya ass? You think I need yo' mama yellin' at me? You know you ain't supposed to drink three coolers in under twenty minutes. What the fuck, Shawna?"

Shawna shrugged both of them off her, almost stumbling down the stairs. "Fuck you, Ronnie," her words spilled in a slow slur. "'Cause of yo' hot ass any one of us could have been shot. Stupid bitch!"

"Girl, you lucky yo' ass drunk and it's yo' birthday." LaRhonda grabbed her arm again, helping her down the stairs.

"Why we walking down these fuckin' stairs?" Keisha asked.

"'Cause if her ass step in the elevator she gonna throw up," LaRhonda replied, annoyed. "How we gonna get her ass sober in two hours?"

"I don't know. But what I do know we all gotta get outta here. I'm sick of this shit. Stupid niggas, stupid bitches." She stopped for a moment and looked at LaRhonda.

"Don't look at me like that. I know what happened. I was there."

"You almost got us in some shit, bitch!" Shawna blurted out.

Keisha and LaRhonda laughed at Shawna's drunken words.

"You know she right!" Keisha continued to laugh.

Finally, after getting Shawna's slow, intoxicated ass to LaRhonda's mother's apartment, they hurried her into LaRhonda's room, then dumped her on the bed. Diamond was with Mary upstairs.

"Why we here?" Shawna slurred.

"'Cause yo' ass drunk as shit and you can't go home like this. We gotta sober yo' ass up quickly; yo' *papi* gonna be callin' soon." LaRhonda laughed.

"Call Vincent. See if he'll go get some coffee and food," Keisha suggested, secretly wanting LaRhonda to leave.

"Now you know he ain't doin' that shit. I'ma have to go get that shit from the chicken spot down the block. Damn, Shawna, fuck it. I'll go get it. Don't fuckin' leave her alone in here," LaRhonda said, pointing to the wall. They all could hear the noise coming from her mother's room.

"I ain't leavin' the room. I don't want to bump into nothin' crazy. Trust me. I think we had enough action for the night." Keisha took a seat next to Shawna on the bed.

Shawna was lying on the bed semiconscious. It was hot out that night and Shawna was wearing a short little sundress; her legs were spread apart and her breasts were almost peeking out the sides of the dress. The room was felt hotter even though the fan was in the window.

Keisha looked at Shawna and couldn't help herself; she gently tested the waters. She called Shawna's name in a whisper. Shawna didn't move. Keisha touched her leg gently. She still didn't move. Slowly she moved her fingers up her inner thigh. Her legs opened wider as if Shawna was inviting her to play.

Keisha wanted to play; she wanted to tell her the truth. Her life was slowly changing; she was meeting new people and evolving into her own skin. Shawna would never admit it, but when they were younger they used to practice kissing on each other all the time. They kept their secret hidden from LaRhonda and as they got older Shawna buried it in her memory, denying it ever happened.

Keisha pulled her hand away.

"I know you want to . . ." Shawna mumbled in a state of mind that was not her own.

Keisha didn't want it this way, but decided she probably would never get another chance like this again. She moved closer to the head of the bed. Bending her head to Shawna's face Keisha placed her lips on hers. Suddenly, she felt Shawna's tongue in her mouth. Keisha's heart pumped with passion as she complied with Shawna's invite.

"Go lock the door . . ." Shawna whispered.

Keisha's mind was in a bliss state; hearing those words only implied she wasn't that drunk. She knew what was going on. *Oh, yes . . . this gonna be good. I can finally be myself. Come clean. Let her know how she really makes me feel.*

"Oh yes, *papi* . . . lick it . . ." Shawna moaned, pushing Keisha's hand toward her hot spot.

Keisha stopped momentarily then whispered, "You want me to play yo' daddy?"

"Yes . . . touch me there, *papi*."

That night Shawna's secret became bigger.

2

Shawna

One year later . . .

"*Mami,* where is my bag?"

"*Aquíes mi hija,*" Shawna's mom replied.

"Ma, you know you have to practice your English if you want that citizenship. So, start talking in English." Shawna was proud that her mom was finally becoming a true American.

"Oh, okay. Umm . . . Keisha, umm called you today."

"Oh yeah, and what she had to say?" Shawna asked, annoyed at the mention of her name.

"Why you act like this? She your best friend, no?"

"Bye, *Mami,* I have to go to work." Shawna kissed her mom on the cheek and walked through the front door. She took the stairs to work out her infuriated mind that Keisha was still pressing her about something that she couldn't even remember. *We been friends way too long for her to be askin' me that shit.*

Shawna quickly exited the building, placing her headphones over her ears so she wouldn't hear anyone trying to get her attention. In a short walk she reached the 3 train, thankful that her train was approaching the station. It was still the morning rush and seats were slim to none, so she stood by the door, nodding to the beat of Jay-Z's *Blueprint* album.

It only took forty minutes to reach Penn Station. Shawna peeked at her watch. *Nine-thirty; damn, I'm late.* Rapidly moving through the crowd, she bumped people out her way with only thing on her mind—her meeting started ten minutes ago. She felt her phone vibrate; glancing at the screen she saw Keisha's name. *That bitch got nerve. I'ma have to see her ass sooner or later.*

Rushing past the security guard at the lobby desk with only a wave, she jumped into the elevator and pressed the button for the fifth floor. Finally, the elevator chimed, alerting her floor. Shawna stepped out and pushed through the glass doors.

"You're late, girl. Mr. Shore here, too," the receptionist said.

"Yeah, I know," Shawna replied, rolling her eyes. She hated how the receptionist always wanted to act like she was actually working instead of trying to give her pussy away to every artist who walked through the door.

It'd been close to six months since her internship became much more at Lifers Music, and she was already feeling the shade of the industry women. They were always trying to either cut her throat or step on her toes. Shawna was the ultimate package: young, beautiful, smart, and willing to work hard for what she wanted. Her once-tiny frame matured into a sexy Latin bombshell measuring nearly five foot nine. Shawna's light brown eyes and long, bouncy reddish hair was envied by most; she was all natural. She silently laughed every time someone walked in with a new weave or extensions when all she had to do was wash and set hers.

The office of Lifers Music was in the midst of it all: Midtown Manhattan, better known as Times Square. She had done her research and making her first connections in New York would definitely lead her to bigger and better things. At first landing the internship was just something to do after school to stay away from temptation by her surroundings. But then it became exciting and the music blew her mind: the latest in hip hop before it even hit the shelves.

Lifers Music was a well-known record label in the music industry when she graduated high school and she immediately enrolled herself at LIU. Applying for an internship at Lifers Music was a joke at first, but when she actually got the call, it became an eye opener to something refreshing and new. After some months her sweet, bubbly personality was well liked. Her knowledge and quick ability to think on her feet led to a permanent position, allowing her to grow within the company.

Shawna rushed passed the conference room and noticed that it was empty. *Hmm, that's strange. I thought there was a meeting.* She rushed to her desk, tucked her purse into a drawer, and checked her Outlook calendar on the computer screen. Confused as to why the conference room was empty she headed back to the reception area. With a smile, she asked Emma, "Did the meeting get cancelled?"

Not wanting to answer her question, Emma pretended she didn't hear her question.

Annoyed at her constant hate Shawna looked around to make sure no one was in view, because her Brooklyn roots were about to show. Shawna slammed her fist against the counter, causing Emma to jump in her chair.

"What the hell?"

"I asked you a fuckin' question, bitch. Are you gonna answer or do you want me to make yo' ass answer?" Shawna couldn't hold her tongue.

"Who do you think you are? You ain't nothin' but a fuckin' errand girl who now gets paid." Emma tried to chop Shawna's ego down.

"No, you must've forgotten who I fuckin' run those errands for." Shawna smiled after catching the reflection of someone getting off the elevator and heading toward the office entrance.

Before Emma could even counter her smart ass she was interrupted by a six foot two, fair-skinned young man with bulging biceps and light-colored eyes. All the hate she had deflated at the site of him.

Shawna rolled her eyes at Emma and wanted to knock her in her head. But instead she beat her at her own game. "Hello, how can I help you?" Shawna flashed her smile.

"Oh, I'm here to see Shore. I had an appointment for nine-thirty, but I got caught up at the airport. I'm with Rich Mafia."

"Okay, why don't you follow me? I can take you to his office." Shawna gestured for him to walk down the hall as she handled Emma quickly. "Now, Emma, I have nothing against you, but if you continue to rub me the wrong way I may have a little birdie whisper in someone's ear about what you do with many of our clients. Executives don't like shit they don't know about. Now do what you were hired for: buzz Mr. Shore and let him know his nine-thirty is heading his way." Shawna hurried down the hall to catch up to the handsome young man.

He couldn't help but to smile at Shawna as she showed him to Shore's office. *She one hella fine. I wonder if I can get her number.* He peeped at her round, plump ass as she stood knocking on Shore's closed office door.

Shawna expected Shore to be in his office; she was wrong, no one answered the knock and the door was locked. Feeling a bit embarrassed she quickly said, "Oh that's right. I'm sorry, I just remembered he wanted you to wait for him in the conference room. Please follow me." She led him to the conference room to wait and offered something to drink. Her face showed smiles on the outside as she left the room, but her insides boiled over approaching Emma. "What the fuck is goin' on?"

"Excuse me? I'm just the receptionist, remember?" Emma asked, continuing with her attitude.

"There you go again. I asked a question. I know what you do."

At that moment the office doors opened with Mr. Shore rushing in. "Good morning, ladies," he said upon entering. He stood at the reception counter when he saw the back of someone's head sitting in the conference room. "Can someone tell me who is in the conference room and why I wasn't called?"

"Well, sir, that's Rich Mafia. I couldn't call you because Shawna here hurried him to your office. If she would have been here on time I could have filled her in on your schedule change this morning." Emma smiled, handing over a few pink slips with messages written on them.

Shore already knew the rules of the office politics between original staffers and any newly hired staff—stay out of it and let them handle their own shit. "Okay, is anyone else here yet?"

"Umm no, everyone is at the Regis Hotel having breakfast with the radio executives about airplay for our clients," Emma answered.

"Everybody?" Shore asked, confused as to why all of the executive staff were at a breakfast meeting.

"Not everybody. Chris and Jena are sick. All the interns are here," she said with a smile.

"Shawna, I will need you in there with me. Go ahead, I will be in shortly." Shore headed to his office to retrieve paperwork off his desk.

Shawna wasn't surprised by Emma's quick reference to her lateness in front of their boss, but she knew just what to do about that. She got real close to Emma behind her desk and lowered her head so their guest couldn't see anything. "Do you really think that bothers me? Do you actually think he cares that I was late? Unlike you I have potential here and you should think about why you still sittin' behind this desk for the past two years. Stupid bitch . . ." Shawna walked into the conference room and waited for Shore to enter.

Three hours of back and forth, phone calls to lawyers, and Shawna's adoring smile and personality got them an exclusive deal potentially making the label millions of dollars in the near future. With over a million hits on WorldStar and buzz about their movement it was a sure hit for the label.

Shawna was all smiles as she walked their new client to the reception area. "It was my pleasure meeting you and I will definitely make sure copies are sent to your lawyer by this afternoon. You have my number so please, if there's anything I can assist you with, I'm just a phone call away. Oh, again, congrats on the baby news. That's wonderful." Shawna waved good-bye as her excitement overwhelmed her. "Oh yeah, oh yeah . . ." Shawna was too inebriated by what just happen to even notice Mr. Shore standing behind her.

"Umm Shawna, can I see you in my office please?" Mr. Shore had a smirk on his face, but it didn't stop Shawna's face from turning plum red. He headed back to his office, giving her a minute to calm herself.

Shawna only hoped that her embarrassment didn't cause any doubt in Shore's mind about her capabilities as a professional. Gathering herself she headed for Mr. Shore's office. Lightly knocking on the office door, scared that her little happy dance was unacceptable to him, she entered, inhaling a deep breath. "Mr. Shore, umm—"

"Please, Shawna, there's no need to be embarrassed. Shit, I was doing the happy dance myself; it was just in my head. That deal just could bring you a promotion and sizeable bump in salary. But there's some things I want to talk to you about before we move too fast. After all, I have to be sure you can handle this life," Shore said, sitting behind his desk.

Shore's words made Shawna stand still for the moment; she didn't know what to expect. Her stomach was in knots as she slowly took a seat in the single chair in front of his desk. The dream of being something big flashed before her. *Don't tell me I just fuckin' ruined everything 'cause of my showin' off in front of that bitch! Fuck, how could I let her get under me like that!* She held the urge to just get up and walk out with the look of shame all over her face.

"First, you were just about perfect in there. I wasn't fully confident that you had it in you, but you definitely showed that assisting Carolyn you learned some things and showed it in your own way. Listen, in order for me to do what I want to do, there are some changes that will have to be made by you." His tone was harsh.

Shawna has heard about these kinds of meetings through the grapevine, but never thought she gave off that energy to even suggest that approaching her would be a sure thing. She definitely wasn't desperate and sure as hell wasn't going to let this motherfucker think she was. "Changes," she said, hinting her building animosity. Her eyes squinted a bit, pulling her head back. *Is he tryin'a do what I think he doin'? Oh, no!*

"What I mean by changes in your life . . . Well, let me put it this way . . . I know you're young, still living with yo' mama, and hanging with yo' old buddies from the hood, which will definitely hold you back. And let's be honest, it really isn't a good look for you if you want to explore your potential," he said with as much sensitivity as he could.

Confused by his soft tone and straightforward words she questioned him slowly. "How do you know I still live with my mama? And how the hell do you know who I hang out with? When I took this job you didn't mention the twenty-four-hour surveillance you apparently got on me. Mr. Shore, I don't mean any disrespect, but I don't think I like the way this conversation is going." Shawna stood up with clenched fists, ready to swing if he tried anything.

"Shawna"—Shore chuckled at her underlying suggestion before continuing—"I ain't tryin'a get in yo' panties like most the executives in this industry. When I see young talent . . . And not the kind of talent young Ms. Emma got out there either." He smiled at her, hoping the crack about Emma would put them on the same page.

When Shawna saw his smile dismissing her uneasiness she felt relieved. After she put away her ghetto attitude she felt a bit silly. His posture never indicated that he was going to force himself on her; she just expected it. She realized that if she really wanted to make it in this business she had to listen to those willing to give her advice. Inhaling a deep breath, she took a seat.

"I'm sorry, Mr. Shore. I just heard about these situations and expected something else."

"First change: call me Shore like everyone else around here. Now I know you might think this may be all too soon, but right now I see what you do. Honestly, from what I see, I think Carolyn is basically making sure all her I's are dotted and T's are crossed by you."

"M . . ." She paused for a few seconds, then continued, "Shore, I can't throw anyone under the bus. Carolyn is great. She took me under her wing and taught me more than what my internship really required of me. I can't say anything bad about her." Shawna wondered where this was leading. *If this man tells me I will be taking Carolyn's job, she could make my life a nightmare in this industry. Oh fuck, what the hell have I got into?*

"You see, that loyalty is what I need to have more of. What if I tell you I'm willing to invest in you and create a new division for you to run?" He raised his eyebrows as he stood and walked over to his small bar, wanting his question to marinate.

Shawna was shocked at his proposal. Exciting thoughts entered Shawna's mind, almost putting her into a trance. *Is this nigga serious? In charge of my own shit? There's gotta be some kinda catch.*

"Umm, did you hear what I just offered you? Shawna, you know this is legitimate right?" He wanted to make sure that this was strictly business and no couch casting was going on. "I know this is a lot of pressure, but I believe in you and I really think your capabilities are far more than being someone's 'cross checker.' I know for sure you can do more than that." He poured some water into a glass and took a sip.

"This is all crazy. I mean I didn't expect all this just from a simple contract signing. I did nothing different. I'm gonna be real right now. This offer smells a little suspect and I'm not sure that I can honestly accept it without all the cards on the table. So, let's move forward six months from now and I"—she paused—"fuck up, what then? Do I lose everything? Or maybe my question to you should be: Can I get a written contract agreeing to terms we both can live with?"

"You see that's why you're being promoted. Keep thinking ahead and you will go far. Now, why don't we get some lunch, and we can discuss this and come to an agreement, and maybe my suggestions won't come off like they did before." He walked toward the door then held it open for her.

Walking past the reception area with Shore felt like the slap Emma needed to be hit with.

This was like a dream to Shawna. Since becoming an employee she put in a lot of unpaid long hours. Finally, someone acknowledged her hard work. Now she only hoped that this lunch was going to end on a good note. By his previous statements she could already guess some of the changes he was going to hint at.

Shawna didn't know how to react to his chivalry; opening car doors, regular doors, asking her what she felt like eating. This was new, especially from one of the bigwigs; not even Carolyn took her out for lunch. Skeptical thoughts forced their way through. *This could be a fuckin' game for real. This nigga could be a fuckin' psycho. Is this really happening?*

Shore could see how his actions could be misconstrued. He definitely didn't want business mixed with pleasure. They both agreed that his choice would be best; after all, Shawna's most expensive taste was Red Lobster. He decided on a quiet little bistro on the Upper East Side of Manhattan.

On the ride over Shawna didn't know whether to be insulted as Shore yapped on his phone or if she should be taking notes of what he was saying. This was surprising and still a bit uncomfortable. Shawna's nerves caused her leg to shake.

She didn't want to say anything to fuck up this opportunity, but her mouth had a mind of its own. Noticing his phone call had ended she quietly said, "Shore, I need you to be straight with me; is this for real?"

"Wow, I can't remember the last time someone asked me that. I may need a drink before we even get there." He chuckled.

"I'd rather not." She smiled then continued, "Drinking alcohol while doing business is never a good idea. No offense of course. I'm sure you've been doing this for years and know the do's and don'ts. You'll have to excuse me if I keep reverting to the same question, but this just seems a little premature for me. Not that I couldn't do it, but I'm so new. Why not offer this to Carolyn? She's been with you much longer than I have." His grin made Shawna's leg twitch a little faster.

Shore knew from the moment he agreed to let her intern it was only a matter of time before she would prove herself a valuable asset to the label. He didn't want any vibes taken the wrong way. "Okay, I'm going to ask you two questions and if you answer yes to both of them you have to accept the promotion and stop implying that this is all some elaborate plan to get your pot of gold." He had to laugh.

Shawna nodded yes with a smile.

"First question, do you like money?" Shore smiled, already knowing her answer.

"I think that's a trick question because of course I would say yes to that. Of course I want more. Of course I want advancement and recognition. Okay, you may fire me after I say this, but I have to know every angle of this 'promotion.' I don't want to be your test subject. The 'newly constructed position to see if it's gonna work' type promotion. Don't build me up to set me on a path of icebergs and polar bears. I hope I'm not too bold, but I don't wanna be anybody's 'risk.' If that's the case then I would like to stay where I'm at for now until I get more experienced."

"You know it kills me when people conjure up the most negative breakdown on something so positive. This could change your life. Look, I'm going to say this as plain as day because I know why you are so skeptical. You are worthy of this position. You have what it takes. This is not 'risk,' as you say. And lastly, I do not want your pot of gold. So can we go have lunch without you asking me that crap again? I am excited to bounce some ideas off you and tell you what should be your next move if you want success." Shore was happy the car was pulling up to bistro; he needed a real drink. This young chick was going to be work, but he knew the outcome would be profitable in the end.

Shawna buried her red face in her hands. Tears almost came to her eyes, feeling embarrassed by her ignorance of a golden opportunity. Shawna allowed all the rumors she heard guide her reactions to Shore's offer. After all he basically confirmed how Emma got her cushy job of receptionist. She wasn't going to let anything or anyone fuck up her shit now. Quickly wiping her eye, Shawna lifted her head and smiled. *This is good!*

After a long lunch and hashing out a three-year contract with great benefits and no casualties to either side, Shawna had a permanent smile on her face. Once she got back from lunch she drew up the contract and presented it to Shore to sign. He sat behind his desk, looked it over as he talked on the phone, and they both signed two copies. Then he placed one in his safe and handed the other copy to her. She began to walk out his office until he held his hand up to stop her.

"Sorry about that, but I had to take that one. It was about headlining a tour in Europe. Oh, how I hate those tours. Aren't you forgetting something?" Shore open his checkbook sitting on top of his desk. He started to write.

Shawna looked confused when he handed her the check.

"Don't tell me you got short-term memory loss. Don't you remember what we talked about?" Shore tilted his head.

"This is a check for fifty thousand dollars. We only discussed rent and car service."

"Yeah, you got a year's rent; car service will be provided by the company, which doesn't come out your personal money. Consider the rest housewarming gifts." At that moment his cell phone buzzed.

Shawna got the hint and headed out the door. She ran to her desk and stared at the check, counting the number of zeros over and over again. It felt like she hit the lotto or she was going to wake up soon; either scenario would change her perception of her future. The buzzing of her desk phone made her realize the check was real. She picked up the phone. "Hello . . ."

"You have a package at the front desk for you," Emma recited.

"Thanks, I'll be right there." She hung the phone up before Emma could say anything smart. She took the check and stuffed it into her purse and headed toward the reception area.

When she approached she could see a huge bouquet of flowers and the company's signature gift of Cristal when contracts were signed. Confused by who would send the flowers, she scrambled to find the card. She pulled out the small envelope buried between the roses and pulled out the handwritten card.

> I'm sorry. I shouldn't have pushed you. Just talk to me.
> Keisha

Emma looked at her. "From yo' boo?"

"Mine yo' fuckin' business," Shawna muttered through her teeth.

At that moment Shore walked into the reception to head out for a meeting. He smiled as he noticed the company's signature gift sitting there.

"Shore, the company messed up and sent this bottle here to Shawna instead of the client this morning. I will get it fixed and hand deliver it tomorrow." She smiled, thinking she was showing how insufficient Shawna was.

"Umm, actually that bottle is for her, Emma. I placed the order myself. When big deals are made it's good to show appreciation. Oh yeah, can you call Carolyn and tell her she needs to meet me at the *XXL* magazine shoot in the morning? Thanks, have a good night. Shawna, you should head home and live a little; after all, this is the first of all the good things to come." Shore walked out the door and headed to the open elevator.

"What the fuck is he talking about, Shawna? No one in this office gets Cristal when deals get made, trust I know. What happened, you worked him over lunch? Ever since you came back from lunch you've been smiling." Emma seemed concerned as to what was going on.

Shawna rolled her eyes and ripped the small card and envelope in her hand. "Can you help me bring this back to my desk, please?"

"Actually I got a dinner date and can't be late. So you'll have to lock up. Thanks. Have a great night." Emma promptly grabbed her purse out the bottom drawer and removed herself from behind the reception desk and headed toward the door.

Shawna couldn't do nothing but smile. She knew by this time tomorrow the news would be obvious. She only hoped that Carolyn wouldn't be on the warpath and out to destroy her career before it really got started. Taking deep breaths as she walked back and forth bringing her stuff to her desk, she realized she wasn't even old enough to drink yet.

Her cell phone buzzed; KEKE showed on the screen. Looking around she made sure that no one was around before she pressed the green ANSWER square on the screen. "Thanks for the flowers, but you didn't have to do that. Listen I had a really good day and I don't want to ruin it by arguing with you about something I can't even remember. Okay, so I don't want to hear 'bout that shit no more. We stopped that shit long time ago."

"A'ight, since you said it like that. I guess my only question would be: What was so good 'bout yo' day? You won the lotto and moving us all out the hood? . . . Please say you did, please, please, please." Keisha giggled.

"Sort of . . ." Shawna slowly said, pulling out her check again.

"When you coming home?"

"I'm leaving now. This is big, KeKe. I wish Ronnie would get out her funk so we can all celebrate. This could change my life. I'll see you soon." Shawna pressed END on her cell phone screen.

After packing up, stashing her bottle, and locking the office, she contemplated telling her girls about her come up. She wasn't even sure she should tell her parents right away. Her twentieth birthday was approaching and she figured she had to cut the umbilical cord sometime so why not now? Shawna was ready to follow her dream.

3

LaRhonda

LaRhonda spent most of her days taking care
of her kids. It'd been a year since the encounter
on the roof between Eric and Vincent. After
that incident it was as if Vincent saw the light;
he stopped hitting on her, moved her and their
kids out the projects, and took care of everything
financially. She didn't have the need for anything. Happiness finally entered her life.

After years of living with her family she was
elated to move out and have a safe and comfortable environment for her kids. When she gave
birth to her oldest, Diamond, she was only seventeen and quit going to school altogether. She
didn't want her drug-addicted mother to take
care of her baby and she definitely didn't want
social services to become a household name for
Diamond. Staying home and doing what she had
to do for her child was her main priority.

When she found out that she was pregnant again she knew staying with her mother would have to change. She pleaded with Vincent and he stepped up. Before she gave birth to her second child, Aaron, Vincent moved them into a small two-bedroom apartment on Bedford and Atlantic Avenue. Knowing what Vincent was doing to make money wasn't a factor; she just knew everything was being taken care of.

After living away from the hell she called home for eighteen years, it only took her eight months to crawl back to her mother. Vincent got caught up in an armed robbery of a popular pizza joint on Utica Avenue. It only took a week to know Vincent's future: five-year bid on the Rock. He took the plea because of the surveillance footage they had as evidence. No paid lawyer would be able to get him out of paying the price for his actions.

LaRhonda cried for days, fighting her regrets and should have's.

Vincent did the right thing by securing her financially for at least two to three months. Every robbery stick-up he survived he stashed some money with his grandmother. Their relationship was close to none, but he knew she wouldn't stab him in the back. One of the calls he made when he got locked up was to her, letting her know that LaRhonda would come by for the money. His grandmother didn't like what he did, but she understood it and blamed the environment his parents raised him in.

LaRhonda isolated herself from everyone and didn't go to retrieve the money until two weeks after Vincent was sentenced. When she finally did get the money, to her surprise there was at least ten grand stuffed into a small knapsack, mostly small bills, but she was thankful she could feed her kids until she signed up for government help. She didn't want to depend on welfare, but her reality was "oh too real" to be risking anything.

She swallowed her pride and worked out a deal with her mother; if her mother kept her company outside she would give her rent money. Knowing that her mother was too old and dried up to be out on the street supporting her habit, she figured providing the means to her inevitable death would be prolonged instead of immediate. She couldn't help loving her mother, but she also couldn't allow her to suffer. Although living there would cause her extreme stress, she had nowhere else to go.

Once she gave the landlord notice, she sold what she could and packed up some suitcases, then headed back to the projects. Upon arrival she placed her kids with an upstairs neighbor she unintentionally grew up with. As she entered her mother's house she could smell the dirt and the faint smell of burning rubber. She pulled out her phone and dialed Keisha's number for the first time since Vincent was sent off to the Rock.

"Hell—"

LaRhonda quickly interrupted her. "I need you and another body to come help me. I'm back at my mother's and I gotta clean this place out before I bring my kids in here. I know we ain't speak in a minute, but I need your help. Can you help?"

"You my girl, right, so you ain't sayin' nothing but a word. I'll be there with reinforcements. Give me an hour." Keisha ended the call.

With a smile on her face she called out to her drunk and high mother, "Yo, Ma?"

A short, bald-headed woman approached her with a small bottle of vodka swinging at her side. "What you want now? You got my money?"

LaRhonda scrunched her nose at the sight of who once was a beautiful woman, Millie. "You know you stink, right? And you know once my kids come in here you gotta do all that shit somewhere else 'cause you won't be getting no money from me. And I sure as hell don't need DFS on my ass."

"Oh, so you wanna play like that. Don't forget who providing these accommodations for your no-good ass. I thought I got rid of your ass, but here you are. Let me guess: his ass either dead or locked up. You can't even keep your man out of trouble." She took a swig from her bottle.

"You know what, here's . . ." She reached into her right jeans pocket and pulled out $250. "That covers two months. Now get the fuck outta here for a while."

Her eyes widened when she saw the green in her daughter's hand. After snatching it from her hand she started to con for more but shut her mouth once she heard a knock at the door.

"Millie, open the fuckin' door. You fuckin' owe me, bitch," a loud, deep voice shouted on the other side of the door.

"Ma, who the fuck is that?" LaRhonda asked with a scared look. *What the fuck am I gettin' into? Shit!*

"I don't know, shit! I owe a lot of motherfuckers!"

Millie's laughter annoyed her to the point of almost slapping her mother down. She contemplated opening the door.

The banging and yelling became louder.

LaRhonda walked into the kitchen, which looked like an ashtray; cigarette butts were smashed all over the counter, table, in the sink, and even on the stovetop. She pulled out a drawer next to the sink; immediately the roaches scattered. She picked up a rusty knife and walked toward the door.

"Bitch, you better open this fuckin' door or—"

LaRhonda swung open the door. "Or what? You better get the fuck outta here before po-po get here, 'cause I already called."

"Who the fuck is you?" The fiend-out addict looked past her and over to her mother. "Millie, tell this bitch to get out my way." He struggled to stay fully awake to attempt his wannabe home invasion.

LaRhonda slammed the door in his face and shouted that the cops were coming, hoping that would send him on his way.

Millie stood there with her bottle in one hand and the only money she had the other. "By the time I get back, I want this house cleaned and them bratty, loud-ass kids you got in your room 'sleep." She walked into her room, slipped into her torn sneakers, and threw a ratty old sundress one size too small over her head. She walked back out toward the door.

"Don't hurry back," LaRhonda insisted.

LaRhonda didn't stop her; she had a lot of work to do before she could bring her kids in

there. Looking around she didn't know where
to start; garbage littered the floor, stains of
whatever were embedded in the carpet, used
needles, used condoms, and liquor bottles, large
and small, were scattered throughout all the
rooms in the three-bedroom apartment.

*First thing first, I gotta go get some working
gloves, latex gloves, garbage bags, and clean-
ing supplies. I better go let Mary know she may
have the kids for more than a few hours. This
shit is crazy. I can't believe I'm back here.*

LaRhonda stood there on the verge of tears. *I
shouldn't be back here. I hate you, Vincent, for
this! Back to one room, ain't this a bitch!* All she
could think of was the horror she left was now
her home once again.

A few hours later, Keisha and two others were
there helping to clear out almost everything;
they ripped the carpet up, and threw out the
sofa, all the dishes and cutlery, along with anything related to drugs and alcohol. She knew
when Millie finally showed up there would be
a fight for throwing out most of her shit. Not
giving a fuck, she continued with the clean-up
without a word.

When Keisha's friends went on another garbage dump behind the building, she finally spoke. "Yo, Ronnie, what's good?"

"What you mean?" Ronnie didn't want to talk about how her life was shit at this point.

"C'mon, I'm your girl. You ain't even call me when Vincent got locked up. Shawna said she called, had her mother call, but you ain't never holla back. You call me out the blue talkin' 'bout you need help. So, what's the deal?" Keisha needed to know.

LaRhonda took a deep breath. "Keisha, me and you have always been straight with each other. So I'ma say it once and then I'ma need you to leave shit alone. Agreed?"

Keisha folded her arms across her chest. "Whateva, Ronnie . . ." She rolled her eyes, waiting for her sorry excuses.

"After Vincent got sent to the Rock"—she paused, not wanting anyone to know how desperate she really was—"I didn't know what to do. I was just going through the motions. Listen, I know I haven't talked to you or Shawna in months and it was like I dropped off the planet, but I was tryin'a make it work with Vin. I wanted him to know I could give up everyone and everything associated with over here including Eric."

"So you stopped talking to us 'cause of that bitch ass. You can't be serious! You lucky I don't give a fuck. You still fuckin' with Eric?" Keisha asked, a bit annoyed that her best friend pushed her to the side because of some man who beat her on the regular.

"Why does that matter?" LaRhonda cut her eyes and sucked her teeth.

"It don't, but are you?"

"Just leave it alone. Why you so concerned anyway? You fuckin' wit' him?" LaRhonda snapped.

Keisha laughed. "Whateva, Ronnie . . ." She pulled off her gloves, threw them in the garbage bag, and said, "I'ma tell Jerome and his boy to help you finish, but I'ma leave now. I gotta go meet up with Shawna and tell her how our friend just returned from the beyond," she lied.

"Don't go spreadin' my business to her either. I'ma see her around sooner or later."

Keisha left without another word.

Oh my God, why she even actin' like that? She don't know what the hell I'm going through. I gotta make shit work right now and I'ma use and do whateva to get what I want. LaRhonda stood there, contemplating her next move.

4

Keisha

"Keisha, what the fuck, I waited for yo' ass like for an hour. Thanks for celebratin' with me. *¡Lagarta!* " Shawna shouted into the phone.

"Celebrate what? Guess who back?"

"My promotion and the fact that I will be movin' out soon . . . Who back?" Shawna wasn't sure who Keisha was talking about.

"Meet me on my floor in ten, in the back staircase," Keisha insisted.

"I ain't meeting you in no back staircase. Last time I did that, fuckin' stupid-ass Jerome walked up on me. You know how pervy he is. Just knock on my door." Shawna hung up the phone. It was time for all that hood stuff to end. If she was going to make those changes Shore mentioned, they would have to start now.

Keisha looked at her phone with her head cocked to the side. *What the fuck is her problem?*

She threw her sneakers back on and headed out her room.

"Keisha, where you going?" her mother asked, sitting at the dining table.

"Um, I'm goin' to the store, you need somethin'?"

Her mother stared at her for moment. "I think we need to talk," her mother said.

"Ma, I ain't—"

"Look, KeKe, you older now and well . . . I need my space. I can't have you walkin' in on me like the other night," her mother interrupted.

"Ma, I told you I was sorry. I didn't remember you sayin' nothin' 'bout havin' company," Keisha said, watching her mother closely.

"KeKe, I can't have that happen again." Her mother's voice turned harsh.

"Ma, you can't be serious. What's really goin' on? Is this 'bout when I cursed whateva his name was the other mornin'?" Keisha's blood was boiling. *I can't believe this shit!*

"Oh, please, I didn't give a fuck. Why can't you stay at that girl's house you had over here the other day?" Keisha's mom sucked her teeth.

"She wasn't nobody, and you know that. Why you comin' at me like this? What happened, yo' new boyfriend don't like me or somethin'?"

"Listen, you causin' me to lose money. You know how this works." Her mother's words were bittersweet.

"Ma, I told you, you don't have to keep doin' that shit. I make—"

"Do you really think that you can make enough money to handle all the shit we want or fuckin' need? Don't be stupid. Now that you older, you can be on yo' own. I don't need you cramping my style," she said, cutting her eyes at her daughter.

"What, you gonna start havin' orgy parties and shit now? Since when you start bringin' that shit home anyway?" Keisha asked with a slight disgust in her voice.

"You don't have a right to ask me that shit. I'm a fuckin' grown-ass woman and I don't gotta explain my business to yo' ass," her mother reminded Keisha.

"Where the fuck am I goin', Ma? You know I can't get no place by myself. Fuckin' one-bedroom apartment like almost a thousand dollars a month." Keisha stood there with her arms folded over her chest.

"Look, KeKe, I need yo' ass outta here by the end of the month," her mother said with some force.

"Ma . . . Ma . . ." Keisha kept calling her, but her mother stood up and walked into her room, shutting her bedroom door behind her.

Her mother's words sliced Keisha's heart like a surgeon—meticulous.

Wow, this is new. Before Keisha blurted out her thought, she hurried out the door, slamming it shut behind her. Filled with anger she walked toward the back staircase, pulling out a cigarette. After a few puffs her anger settled for the moment. It'd been three years since she left school, got her GED, and busted her ass to get a job and help out. Never did she think her mother would turn on her because of some bullshit she wanted to do. *I'm the one who kept shit goin' when she wasn't doin' nothin'. This ungrateful bitch!*

When Keisha turned thirteen her mother's big job in the city wasn't a family secret anymore. Unfortunately, it became known by everyone in the hood. The night of her birthday party Keisha's mother got real drunk and propositioned most of the men on the arms of her friends' moms. When she returned to school Keisha had her first fight, because some girls were talking about her mother hoeing herself out to any man. It infuriated her that her mother didn't care why she had the fight. Her mother was more upset that she had to stay home because of Keisha's week suspension from school.

A buzzing noise alerted her. SHAWNA flashed across the screen. Keisha sent the call to voice mail. "Fuck that shit, I ain't tryin' to hear 'bout nobody fuckin' accomplishments when I need a place to stay before the end of the week is out," she said out loud to herself.

Scrolling through her contacts her thoughts were negative. *Fuck, I screwed over half these chicks in here. Who the fuck I'ma gonna call to save me now?* Keisha's phoned buzzed again.

"Where the fuck you at?"

"Shawna, some shit just went down so I ain't comin' through. I'ma—"

Confused by Keisha's response Shawna interrupted, "What the fuck happened? Did somebody die or some shit?" Shawna let out a nervous laugh.

Pissed off that Shawna felt it was okay to laugh when Keisha's tone was nowhere close to joking she blacked on her. "Bitch, what the fuck you laughin' at? You think you so fuckin' perfect. Your shit stink just as much as anyone else in this motherfuckin' hood. Do you know how many times I saved yo' ass from gettin' an X marked on yo' face? Nobody don't wanna hear nothin' 'bout yo' good fuckin' news."

"KeKe, what the fuck did I do? You said you was comin' to see me. You know what, fuck this shit. I don't need you or Ronnie as my so-called friends anymore. Y'all don't like nothin' good for nobody else but yo'self. Fuck you!" Shawna hung the phone up.

Keisha's phone buzzed again. She picked up without looking at the screen, expecting Shawna to be on the line. "Why don't you go fuck yo' daddy again, bitch!"

"Whoa . . . Keisha?" a female voice asked.

"Who this?"

"It's Nicole. Is this a bad time? Sounds like you in the middle of something."

"Nicole . . . Nah, it's all good. What's up?" Keisha asked, trying to suppress her anger.

"Umm, thought maybe you could swing by tonight and we could finish what we started. Besides, some of my girls want to meet you," Nicole replied.

"Meet me? Why? I told you I'm not out there like that. I don't wanna meet yo' friends." Keisha's anger resurfaced.

"Damn, so what was all that talk about the other night? You said you were ready. You still scared about what other people going to say? Keisha, I told you I would help you get over your fear. Besides, who the fuck really cares about who you have in your bed anyway?"

Keisha took a deep breath. "Fine, but I don't wanna meet yo' friends. Or at least not yet. I'll be there later."

"Well, I guess that's better than nothing. I'll see you like in an hour?"

"Yeah." Keisha pressed END on her iPhone. *It can't be that bad. I gotta meet 'em sometime, might as well start now,* her thoughts rolled in.

5

Shawna

Shawna's mind was racing. She lay on the bed in her room, looking at her phone. *Should I call? Why should I call? Oh my God, I can't believe she played me like that, of all people—me. I can't fuckin' believe her. What the fuck was her problem? I'm so tired of both they asses, I swear. They don't know any better than what they were taught and they weren't taught much, like most of these girls living in these projects.*

She was in a good place and no matter how she tried to fight it she couldn't just shut them out. When she was younger LaRhonda and Keisha were the first girls to talk to her when she moved into the projects. Keisha only befriended her because of LaRhonda, but it didn't matter; she talked and played with Shawna. They were always together; if you saw one the others were next to or close behind. As they were growing up Keisha and LaRhonda had it all. Every week they both had something new in the latest fashion, footwear, and the newest hairstyle out. Shawna always envied their style and closeness. All the gossip about them both didn't make her shy away from them; it only made her want their friendship even more.

Staring at her phone, she remembered when she was about eleven and her parents weren't home when she arrived from school one afternoon. Thinking LaRhonda would have no problem having her hang out at her house until her parents came home she knocked on her door. She never thought it would be the wrong thing to do. Shawna closed her eyes.

"Hi, Mrs. Miller, is LaRhonda home?" Shawna didn't realize at the time her disheveled look and twisted lips were because she was drunk and high on crack.

"Who you? What you want?" Millie leaned against the open door in a short tiger-print teddy, showing all her goods and slurring her questions.

Millie was loud in yelling for LaRhonda. After a minute she could see LaRhonda behind her.

"Shawna, what you doing here?" She was surprised that she was at the door. After years

of knowing each other she never once got invited over.

"Shawna? Oh you the super daughter. Tell yo' daddy he can come on by—" Millie tried to get her words out.

"Ma, shut the fuck up. Shawna, what's up?" LaRhonda shoved her mother to the side and stepped out into the hall.

Millie stumbled to balance herself. *"Bitch, stay the fuck out!"* She slammed the door shut.

Shocked at Millie's actions, Shawna was confused. LaRhonda portrayed her mother as the best. It was clear she wasn't. *Why would she lie to me? I thought we were friends.*

Before LaRhonda could say anything, someone opened the door. A man stood there, tall, skinny, with red pus-like blotches all over his face, scabs on his neck and arms. Creepy wasn't the word or even close to it as he stood before them, showing his rotten teeth.

Who the hell is that? He can't be related. Shawna couldn't believe her friend knew him.

"Why you out here? Get your ass in this house. What the fuck I done told you 'bout talkin' to yo' mother like that?" he asked, indicating his annoyance.

Without hesitation Shawna quickly pulled on LaRhonda's hand and whispered, *"Ronnie . . ."*

She stared at LaRhonda, waiting for her to say something brave. Shawna was uneasy, but knew that LaRhonda would protect her like she always did.

Embarrassed by Shawna's reaction she slowly said, "He's my father."

Shawna stepped back. How can this be? "I thought you said your father was dead," she said, revealing the ultimate lie in front of him. Afraid of what LaRhonda would do or say she quickly said, "Sorry, I—"

"Why are you here anyway?" LaRhonda asked, irritated.

"I'm locked out. No one is home," she said with her eyes fixed on her angry father.

"Where yo' daddy at?" LaRhonda's father asked.

"Well, you can't stay here. Let me call Keisha and see if she home. I'll be right back." LaRhonda cut her eyes at her father, walking past him, whispering, "Go smoke some more shit, crack-head."

Before she made it two steps, he snatched LaRhonda by her fake ponytail and slammed her face up against the open steel door.

Water built in her eyes, but not one tear rolled down her cheek. More humiliated by his appearance, and that, since Shawna knew, *everyone at school would know, she shouted back, "What the fuck? Leave me alone."*

Shawna watched in horror as he shouted and slapped her around. She wanted to run and get help, but dared not to. Instead she slowly backed away, hoping she could just remove herself from the situation.

"Where the fuck you think you goin'?"

Shawna began to shake. One thought entered her mind: My father will kill you if you lay a hand on me.

LaRhonda jumped in front of Shawna. "Don't touch her, she ain't yo' child!"

He raised his hand to strike her again, but stopped when Millie opened her mouth. "Why you even out here fuckin' with these kids? I need some; you know I can't do that shit by myself. Why you always gotta cause fuckin' trouble, Ronnie?"

LaRhonda looked at Shawna. "Let's go."

"Yeah, bitch, go where somebody actually cares 'bout yo' ass!" Millie slammed the door after pulling LaRhonda's father inside.

Shawna and LaRhonda never talked about what happened or even why she lied about her father. She could only remember LaRhonda threatening to destroy her social life if she ever said a word about the incident. At that time she was just coming into her coolness and having friends to protect her was most important; most females disliked her because they were jealous.

Sitting up in her bed after her memories spun in her mind, Shawna decided to give Keisha a call anyway and send LaRhonda a text. She looked at the time on her phone: 1:31 A.M.

Hey, Ronnie. If u up call me.

Shawna already knew LaRhonda probably wouldn't text her back. She dialed Keisha; the phone rang a couple of times until she heard her voice mail. She didn't want to leave a message. Within a few seconds after hanging up, her phone buzzed with Keisha's name flashing across the screen. Shawna picked up the phone. "Keisha . . ." Hearing muffled movement she didn't know if it was a butt dial.

She listened for a moment, and a faint female's voice asked a question. "Why don't you want to come out?" Before hanging up the phone she heard Keisha's voice clearly. "I don't want to tell every Tom, Dick, and Mary that I am fuckin' gay, Nicole. Why can't you just understand that?"

Shawna let out a loud gasp. Then the phone disconnected. *What the hell was Keisha sayin'? Who was Nicole?*

RONNIE CALL ME ASAP

Shawna sent the message but didn't know if she would reply.

6

Keisha

"Touch it, it ain't gonna bite . . ." Nicole whispered a low voice in the dark bedroom.

"I don't know if I like it this way . . ."

"Don't you want it?"

With the feeling of her nectar trickling down her leg, Keisha licked her lips and reached out in front of her.

"See I told you it wouldn't bite. Glide your hand up and down slowly. Keep your eyes closed," whispered Nicole, kneeling on the bed with Keisha's naked body lying between her legs.

As Keisha glided her hand up and down the well-lubed, warm rubber ten-inch cock over her, Nicole's soft fingertips rubbed on her hard nipples, causing her to moan and pull on her strap-on.

"You like that? You want to taste it?"

Keisha pulled Nicole closer by the strap-on; to her surprise it looked like it was glowing. Keisha eased up suddenly. "What the fuck is this?"

"It's my Henry; he glows as you get hotter." Nicole smiled. "That's why I told you to close your eyes first. He needs to be warmed up first."

Keisha smiled and lay back down into her previous position. Nicole spit on Henry's slightly neon green glowing head. Slowly Nicole outlined Keisha's lips with the tip before allowing her to lick it. Bit by bit Keisha opened her mouth to allow Henry warmth. Nicole swayed her hips back and forth, watching Henry's glow become stronger.

"You like him in your mouth? The faster you go the more he glows . . ." Nicole giggled.

"Two tongues would be better . . . Take him off . . ."

Nicole took Henry off then laid her smooth, pale body beside Keisha. Then she placed her ten-inch glowing Henry between them and enticed Keisha to suck on it together. Their tongues fought for each other and Henry's solid tip. Keisha's hand easily reached down to Nicole's wetness and rubbed on her swollen clit.

"Yeah, baby, touch it . . ."

Keisha held Henry by his base and teased Nicole's tongue with him. She watched as the neon glow disappeared over and over again. Keisha's sexual drive exploded; she took Henry, strapped him on, and opened Nicole's legs far apart. Lowering her head she slowly kissed Nicole's naked body until she hit her sweet spot. Stroking Henry's head, she moved her tongue rapidly against Nicole's flesh.

"Oh yes . . . faster . . ." Nicole screamed out wrapping her legs over Keisha's shoulders.

Keisha picked up her head and quickly put Henry to work. She pushed until she didn't see any glowing light.

"Ahhh . . . you fuckin' bitch . . ." Nicole shouted.

Keisha pumped faster, holding Nicole's legs up by her ankles. The feeling was amazing; it was control and passion she never felt before with anyone. It was the best of both worlds.

"Oh yes, make him fuck me harder . . . I want to cum . . ." Nicole cried out.

Keisha tried to hold her shaking legs up, but couldn't. Instead she pushed her legs back toward Nicole's head, exposing her wet flesh even more. Keisha lowered her body and drove Henry deep into Nicole again. Her moans and struggles turned Keisha on more and more as she pumped forcefully into Nicole.

"Yes, yes, yes . . . make my pussy hurt . . . I like it like that . . ."

Keisha pulled Henry out and motioned for Nicole to get on all fours. "Henry wants it from behind now."

Nicole's eyes widened, surprised at Keisha's request, not knowing if this was a breakthrough in Keisha's comfort with her sexuality. Nicole didn't hesitate and got on all fours, excitingly pushing her small, perfectly rounded ass out as far as she could. *Times like these are worth all the pain and money I spent on those butt injections,* she thought, looking at her dimmed reflection in the mirrored headboard of her bed.

Keisha slapped her ass, watching the bounce. She was disappointed that Nicole's ass did not jiggle or wiggle like most girls she's seen in her porn movies. Keisha slapped her again, but harder. Nicole jerked a bit.

"Give me Henry . . ." Nicole moaned, playing with her hot spot.

Keisha teased her with it, outlining her outer lips then dipping into her slightly over and over again. She could see Nicole's excitement about to burst so to put her over the top, Keisha bowed her head and stuck her tongue deep inside her, causing all her juice to spill over. Feeling her climax made Keisha want more; quickly she pushed Henry in and fucked Nicole harder and stronger until she reached her pivotal moment.

After another hour of playing with her new friend Henry with Nicole, Keisha collapsed on the bed out of breath. "Oh shit!"

Nicole's head was touching the floor and the lower part of her body was still on the bed. She tried to pull herself up, but she was too weak. Looking up at the ceiling she could see the sunrise's light peeking through from the tops of the window. "Keisha, help me," she called out, reaching out.

"I . . . can't . . . move." Keisha's words were slow and broken, almost retarded.

Nicole laughed as she rolled the rest of her body off the bed and stood up. "I told you I would put that fear out of you. So now you know what you want, right?"

Keisha raised her head. "What is that supposed to mean?"

"Nothing, I mean . . . You hungry?" Nicole stopped the questioning and changed the subject.

"What time is it? Where the hell is my phone?" Keisha slowly turned over and allowed her legs to hang off the bed.

"Umm, it's about five-something; the sun is starting to come up. I'm going into the shower then I'll fix us some breakfast," Nicole said, picking up Keisha's phone and clothes off the floor, then setting them on the edge of the bed.

Keisha reached for her phone because the notification light was blinking. She missed a few calls so she touched RECENTS for the call list to appear. "What the fuck?" Standing up she scrolled through the list.

Ronnie 3 Missed Calls
Shawna Outgoing 20 Seconds
Shawna Incoming 2 Seconds

Her heart pumped faster. "I didn't call her. Fuck, I wonder . . ." Keisha touched her text inbox on the screen of the phone. There were two messages from LaRhonda.

Bitch u need to ans yo phone
Where u at?

"She must've heard somethin'. Ain't no way Ronnie gonna be callin' my ass like that for some bullshit. Fuck! How the hell I'ma explain this shit?" Keisha said to herself, rushing to put her clothes on. Hearing the shower still running Keisha headed for the door. She didn't care what Nicole would have to say later. Keisha shut the door behind her and bypassed the elevator for the stairs. When she got to the front door she looked at herself quickly, making sure there were no white residue marks on her face. She threw her hood over her head and walked toward the train station on 125th Street and Lenox Avenue to head home.

She got onto the train and sat back in her seat, hating that her secret was finally in the forefront. Keisha was built like an athlete; strong and muscular. She had light skin, smooth short hair, with light brown eyes, total opposite of her mother. Her appearance at times could be misconstrued. From week to week her look changed; tight pants with high boots to hoodies and sweats. Thinking back to what confirmed her path made it easier for her to digest her imminent reality.

"It's your turn." Keisha nudged her.

"I don't wanna play this no more," Shawna moaned.

"Well, what you wanna do?"

"I'ma tell you something, but you have to promise not to tell anyone. Okay?" Shawna asked.

"Tell me . . ." Keisha begged.

"I saw Tyrek in the hallway today and we almost kissed but . . ."

"But what?" Keisha started to giggle.

"I didn't do it because I . . . I . . . don't know how," Shawna said, embarrassed by her inexperience.

"So that's why you shoulda kissed him." Keisha sat closer to her. "All you have to do is pucker up like this . . ." She poked her lips out.

"No, I wanna learn how to do it." Shawna looked at Keisha. "Umm . . . don't think of me funny but can you teach me?"

Keisha laughed. "Ahh, Shawna, I'm a girl!"

"So . . . You've done it before. I've seen you with what's his name every day right before fourth period lunch. Y'all look like experts in my eyes. C'mon, KeKe, we ain't gonna tell nobody. It'll be our little secret," Shawna said, trying to convince Keisha.

"Okay, just once." Keisha got up and closed her bedroom door. "Stand up."

Shawna stood up with excitement and faced her. She was a little taller than Keisha so it was a bit awkward.

"Okay, I'm just gonna do it and you follow what I do. You ready?" Keisha looked up at Shawna's beautiful eyes and flawless skin.

There was something different Keisha felt when their lips touched. It was softer, nicer, and much sweeter than her little fling make-out sessions in the schoolyard at lunch. Instead of fresh Doritos Ranch chip breath, it was bubble-gum luscious. Goosebumps trickled down her arms and for the first time someone else made *it tingle down there. From that day forth Keisha always hinted at a practice session when they were alone. Their little secret survived middle school, but once they got to the seventh grade, Shawna decided she was an expert and wanted her to show off her capabilities to every boy who showed her attention.*

The sudden movement of the train shook her out her flashback. She still had that feeling for Shawna, and felt she had to come clean to her to preserve their friendship. Keisha wanted Shawna in her life, as a friend or more, she didn't care. *It was she who made me see what I really wanted*, she admitted silently. She stood up to exit as the train pulled into the station.

It was bright outside and too early in the morning to see anybody hanging about. Her phone was buzzing. *It's probably Nicole. I'll talk to her later.* She entered her building and headed for the staircase. With her mind flooded with emotions and thoughts, she climbed slowly four floors up. When she opened the door to exit the staircase she saw her mother kissing an older man good-bye. Quickly she closed the door back and listened for her mother to close the apartment door. *Fuck, I didn't think she was gonna be up!*

Keisha heard the apartment door slam closed. She waited another five minutes before opening the exit door again. Walking toward the door she pulled out her keys, then unlocked the apartment door. The smell of liquor and sex still lingered in the air from her mom's previous activities. It was dark in the house, despite the morning brightness outside. In a few steps she bumped into something hard. *What the hell is my bike doing in the hallway?* Walking a few more steps forward she bumped into something else. *What the fuck is this shit?*

When she flicked on the light switch she let out a gasp. Boxes labeled with her name, large black garbage bags, her bike, her TV, and a couple of suitcases littered the hall, spilling over into the living room. She hurried to her room and pushed the door open. When she turned the light on she saw that her room was no longer her room. Her bed, dresser, and TV stand were still there. *This bitch is buggin'! She can't do this to me now.*

Keisha's anger became known. "Ma, wake the fuck up. Why is all my shit out my room?" she screamed at her mother's bedroom door.

She heard no movement. Keisha banged on the door. "Wake the fuck up!"

Her mother finally unlocked the door. "What?"

"Why is all my shit in the fucking hallway?"

"What the fuck you mean why is all your shit in the hallway? We spoke about this, Keisha. You need to leave. I was about to just put you shit outside so be fuckin' happy you got shit." Her mother yawned. "Listen I already spoke to Mr. Vasquez and he said he could keep yo' stuff in the basement until you ready to come get it. The locks gonna change, too, by the end of the week." She closed her door, not waiting for any response from her daughter.

Keisha wanted to kick the door in and choke her mother out with all the betrayal and anger she was feeling. Instead she went to the kitchen, and emptied all the liquor from the bottles lined up on top the fridge. Then she looked under the kitchen sink and pulled out the metal mesh covering the rat hole. She walked into the living room and picked up the heavy glass ashtray and smashed it against the TV.

The loud crash made her mother rush into the living room. "Keisha, what the fuck are you doin'?"

"I ain't leavin' on good terms since you wanna do it this way," Keisha yelled.

"Oh, so you also want handcuffs on your wrists, too, huh? You think you can break my shit and get away with it? Who the fuck do you think you are? You don't run shit up in here. Don't make me call the police."

"After all the shit I done did for you, you gonna do me like this. Like some fuckin' trick off the street. I'm your daughter. I left school early and got a job just so we could eat. Now you kickin' me out 'cause I walked in on you and some random motherfucker?" Keisha didn't want to believe that her mother could be so cruel.

When her mother stopped going into the city there was no money coming into the house. It was as if her mother couldn't bear to show her face outside since her trickin' ways were exposed. That's when she starting allowing tricks into her home, but the only setback was her clients weren't the old, rich white dudes who showered her with gifts. Her clients now sported missing teeth, exact change, and barter haggling skills—"give me this and I'll give you that."

Keisha worked most days and was out most nights. Her mother's company was never a problem until lately; it was more frequent and at all hours of the day or night. Leaving her mother's house never entered her mind, but now it seemed necessary. She looked at the broken glass on the floor and the smashed TV screen on the wall.

"You need to go now!"

Keisha stared at her mother with disgust and rage. "You ain't shit! You shoulda dropped my ass off with my father."

Those words infuriated Keisha's mother. "Your father?" She laughed. "Let me let you in on a secret . . . I don't know who your father is. Why don't you go find him?"

Keisha's heart sank. *She doesn't know who my father is? Is she just sayin' that?* She walked closer to her mother and back-smacked her.

With her face burning her mother shouted, "Get the fuck outta here! I don't ever wanna see your sorry ass 'round here again!" She rushed into her room, holding her face and slamming the door behind her.

Keisha stood there, regretting her actions. She looked around, dropped her keys on the coffee table, and emptied the knapsack lying on the floor. She shoved in it what was important to her: some clothes and paperwork. On the way out she took her bike and exited the apartment. Leaving the rest of her stuff didn't matter; it was all junk now: pictures, books, clothes, and small reminders from her childhood. *Fuck it,* she thought, walking out the door.

Her phone buzzed when she reached the outside of the building. Keisha pressed ANSWER. "Hey what's up?"

"What happened to you this morning? You just left without sayin' nothing. What's the deal with that?" Nicole unleashed.

"Nicole, I just got kicked out my house. I had to leave to come get my bike or else I can't work. So if this is one of those calls where you get all fuckin' loud and shit I don't need it." She sighed.

"Oh shit . . ." Nicole felt stupid. "I'm sorry. Are you okay?"

"Nicole, I don't need to answer stupid questions either," Keisha snapped back.

"Why don't you just come back over here? You can stay with me until you figure something out. I promise it'll be fun. Okay?" Nicole encouraged.

"I don't know 'bout that. I ain't . . . I'll call you." Keisha ended the call.

With no stability her thoughts were rattled. *How the fuck I'ma pull this shit off now? Now who do I call? Shawna? LaRhonda? Where the fuck am I gonna go? Fuck it.*

Keisha rode her bike to the corner store and used the ATM. She retrieved enough money for a hotel room for the night.

7

LaRhonda

"Fuck this shit. I can't do this no fuckin' more. I can't be truckin' up here with these fuckin' kids and yo' ass wanna do this shit to me," LaRhonda mouthed off loudly so everyone around could hear.

"Ronnie, calm the fuck down, man. I don't need yo' ass actin' crazy right now." Vincent's tone was low and gritty. He tried to hold on to Aaron a bit longer.

LaRhonda started to gather her things and pulled her kids away. She was mad as hell. When she signed the visitors log before going through security she saw another female's name and it wasn't his mother. La-Rhonda knew the name; it was from their past. "What the fuck, Vincent? Since when she start comin' up here? How she even know you here? That only means you was fuckin' talkin' to her ass when you got in here.

You ain't been here but so long. You must think I'm fucking stupid, Vincent." LaRhonda's hands started shakin'; she wanted to slap the shit out of him, but getting arrested wasn't her plan.

"That bitch don't mean nothin'. You go 'head on with that bullshit. I don't care 'bout that bitch! You see I ain't callin' you for no commissary. Why you trippin'? She plays her role. She ain't said nothin' to you 'bout nothin' so ain't no reason for all this." Vincent had to control his anger; he just came out the hole for catching wreck on some dude for playing around with him. He sat there with a straight face and his hands on the table, eyeing the CO on watch. Hearing his kids crying and Ronnie acting up, he nodded to the CO.

There was an underlying understanding between inmates and COs when they were on visits. When the visiting guest starts to fly off the handle, two nods gets the inmates out of there to prevent any more added time to their sentence—in most cases something always goes wrong. Most COs were cool about it, but there were those who wanted inmates to wild out. The CO walked over with a grin. "Let's go."

"What the fuck you smirkin' at? C'mon, Diamond, say bye to yo' daddy 'cause you ain't gonna see his ass no more. Stupid-ass motherfucker!" LaRhonda took hold of Aaron and stomped out with Diamond slowly following her. "Diamond, I said c'mon!"

LaRhonda held her tears while walking out the building and toward the bus idling to return to Queens. Diamond looked at her and asked, "Mommy, why we can't go back to see Daddy?"

"Diamond, just be quiet and sit there. We don't need yo' no-good daddy. You got me and yo' brother." LaRhonda sat back and stared out the window, losing herself in her thoughts. *How could he do this do me? He knows how I feel 'bout that bitch. Did he not think I was gonna see the visitors log? Fuck that nigga; he ain't doin' shit for me or his kids right now. I can't believe he would even talk to that bitch after she did what she did! He can have that crazy stalker bitch. To think I beat that bitch's ass every single time she was in the vicinity, almost getting locked up for it, too. But this is how he repays me? Fuck this bastard!*

She pulled out her phone and sent a text. Can we talk?

Yeah, was the reply received.

Meet me at the train station in an hr

One minute later a text alert chimed.

A'ight. I'll be there.

She knew what she had to do. *It won't be hard to convince him.*

The last time she spoke to Eric was when she returned to her mother's house. He found out that she was back and called her to smoke some weed and to catch up. She didn't understand why he was so stuck on her. LaRhonda cheated on him, played him for a fool, then almost got his ass killed by her baby daddy. With her kids beside her, LaRhonda stepped off the train and walked toward the exit in a hurry. It was thirty minutes past the initial time she told Eric to meet her. *I hope this fool ain't leave!*

"Hello, beautiful, what's your rush?" Eric asked, walking up behind her.

"Mommy, I'm hungry." Diamond tugged on LaRhonda's hand.

"Diamond, I'ma fix you somethin' when we get back to the house. Now be quiet," LaRhonda snapped.

Eric wasn't surprised at LaRhonda's response to Diamond. "Why don't we go to my house?"

"How we all goin' to yo' house, Eric? C'mon be serious." She rolled her eyes at him.

"I told you my moms left for Florida. She ain't comin' back. It's just me now. Didn't I tell you that?" Eric smiled.

"And you want us"—she motioned her hand to her kids and herself, mirroring Vanna White's actions—"all of us to come to yo' house?"

"I ain't askin' you again. If you don't wanna go that's on you." Eric turned to walk down the stairs to the street level.

"Eric, don't you gotta get on the train to go to yo' house?"

"I don't ride on trains anymore. I'm takin' a cab," he responded quickly.

LaRhonda pulled on Diamond's hand with Aaron on one hip and followed Eric like a lost puppy dog.

Before reaching his house he picked up some Chinese food for LaRhonda and the kids. After stuffing their faces, LaRhonda's kids were fast asleep in his mom's old room while they hung out in the living room.

"What happened today?" Eric asked, rolling up a blunt.

"You better open that window and put a towel down by the door before you spark that. Don't forget my kids in here."

"Nah, we gonna just go out into the staircase for 'bout twenty minutes. 'Em kids ain't wakin' up, trust me." He put his final lick on the blunt and walked toward the door. "You comin'?"

LaRhonda stood up with a cheesy smile on her face and followed him through the door and into the staircase.

"So what's the deal, Ronnie?"

"Umm, you know I'm sorry for what I did and all that stupid shit that happened with Vincent. I know—"

"Aaron's mine, ain't he?" Blowing smoke O's into the air, he smiled then passed her the blunt. He knew what she was about to say; after all, he had suspicions the entire time, just never acted on them.

LaRhonda almost choked; he beat her to it.

"Be careful now, that's some strong shit. Pass that here." Eric took the blunt out of her hand.

She stared into Eric's eyes. "How . . . Umm, when did you come up with that?"

"C'mon now, I know the real story. You was still fuckin' me when he thought he was only fuckin' you. If I remember correctly, we fucked just about every day that month straight." He passed her the blunt again.

"How did you know I was still fuckin' him? I was with you almost every day."

He smiled. "That nigga don't know how to keep his mouth shut."

"What you mean by that?" LaRhonda's brow arched.

"You know when niggas get around niggas and how shit go. There's always that one louder than everyone else. You know how he is. I don't have to explain his ways to you. I know he got a small bid to do. Why you think I called you? I gave you your space when he moved your ass to Atlantic and Bedford. I left you alone after you embarrassed me on that roof. That nigga had a hell of a time with that shit. It took me a month to start comin' 'round here again. You was right; fuckin' with 'em dime-bag hustlers wasn't doin' shit for me." He took the last pull off the blunt and flicked it against the wall.

"Wait, hold on . . . Let me find out you actually doin' somethin' now." LaRhonda twisted her lips to the side, watching him carefully.

"Yeah, you could say that. I gotta know if Aaron my kid or not." Eric exited the staircase and entered the apartment.

LaRhonda walked into the apartment and headed straight for the bedroom to check on the kids.

"Still 'sleep, right?" Eric asked sitting on the sofa.

"Yup, it don't even look like they moved any." She sat there with a tight feeling against her chest. She didn't want to admit it, but he was right. LaRhonda had no idea who fathered Aaron.

"A'ight, Ronnie, let's handle this like adults. Let's go take a DNA test tomorrow. I'll catch all the ends. After that we can see what happens. In the meantime, I think you should stay here with me. I can't have you and my ki . . . I mean your kids staying in that fucked-up house with yo' mom. I ain't tryin'a hear that 'em kids ain't with you 'cause of yo' mom. That's on some real shit, you hear me?" Eric watched for her response.

"So, what, I'm just supposed to pack my shit up and move in with you? What if you ain't the father? Are you gonna kick my ass out then? You gonna take care of us? All of us? Ain't no man tryin'a do that. C'mon, Eric, tell me why you really want me here."

"Ain't nobody puttin' a gun to yo' head. You got a choice." Eric inched closer to her on the sofa. "I truly care about you and what happens to you. I've seen all the shit you been through. You need something good in your life. Besides that boy Aaron look just like my ass." He smiled at her, hoping she would agree.

Tears filled her eyes. *This can't be happening. Why does he want to do this?* She couldn't hold back her sobs. For the first time since Vincent got locked up she actually had hope for her future. "Thank you," she said through sobs and sniffles.

DNA? LaRhonda's tears covered her uncertainty, but she was going to sop up all he would give. After pulling on his heart strings a little more with Vincent's latest slap in the face, her cunning mind tricked him into picking up her things by her mother's house and bringing them back. Handing him over the keys to her mother's house was easy; she didn't want to show her face around there if she didn't have to. Eric left her to herself.

After he left, she looked around the apartment. She'd been there before, but never by herself. Snooping was her favorite hobby and she had nothing but time on her hands. Opening cabinets, drawers, looking through the mail left on the table; she looked through every nook and cranny and found nothing out of the ordinary. He was straight up; no guns and no drugs.

LaRhonda's phone buzzed on the coffee table, causing her to jump. "Oh shit," she gasped, holding her chest. She walked over and picked up the phone. "Hello?"

"Ronnie, it's me, Shawna . . ."

"Let me guess, you callin' me to ask me why I ain't call you when I came back, blah, blah, blah . . ."

Shawna twisted her lips. "Didn't you get my text the other night?"

"No," LaRhonda lied. She didn't want to be bothered by her shit at one-thirty in the morning.

Shawna couldn't understand what her problem was; she knew Ronnie was lying. "Okay, did you know Keisha was gay?"

LaRhonda smiled and played the role. "What? No way . . . What you talkin' 'bout?"

Shawna could sense she was missing something. "Did she tell you she was?"

LaRhonda couldn't keep her chuckles quiet; her sarcasm leaked more. "Shawna, you can't be serious. Are we talkin' 'bout our KeKe?"

"Oh, so that's how it goes after so many years. You of all people should know better. I helped you . . . my mother helped you, even my father, now you and Keisha wanna act like y'all don't want nothin' to do with me. What the fuck did I do to y'all?" Shawna voiced with a harsh temper to match. She tried to calm herself, awaiting a rapid response from Ronnie.

LaRhonda was shocked by the conviction of her words; it seemed she actually meant it. She sat there in silence on the phone. LaRhonda's jaw dropped at the sound of the click. *Ain't nobody need her ass. Ghetto? She wasn't callin' nobody ghetto when we was beatin' the shit outta bitches for her. Boogie-ass bitch! She was never part of my hood anyway!* LaRhonda picked up her phone and sent a text.

Yo KeKe guess who ain't our friend no more? LOL

She sat there for a few minutes, waiting for Keisha's reply, but never received anything. Just as she was about to dial her number there was a knock at the door. *I didn't say where I was at to nobody,* she thought, tiptoeing to the door. She stood on her toes and looked through the peephole. *What the fuck is he doin' here?*

"LaRhonda, I know you in there. Just open the door. Eric sent me with some of yo' shit."

LaRhonda unlocked the door and asked, "Why he sent *you* of all people?"

"You gonna help or just run yo' mouth? Some of yo' shit still by the elevator so I suggest you move and let me do what I got to do before yo' shit start disappearin'." He moved past her with a box of toys.

"That ain't mine . . ." Looking in the box after he put it on the floor, she saw that the toys were still in packages. "Shotta, this ain't my shit. You didn't steal this shit?" Her eyes widened like a kid on Christmas Day.

"You did it again. You done got him to fall for yo' dog-and-pony show again. I just hope you ain't teachin' yo' daughter that shit," he said, turning toward the door to retrieve the rest of the stuff by the elevator.

"You just mad I ain't let you hit it twice. I'm sure that's the norm for you. Lawd knows how many groupies you done ran through every time you book some damn studio time." She stuck her middle finger up in the air. LaRhonda didn't care what he called her; all she could think of was how was she going to get out this DNA test Eric got set up in the upcoming days.

After Shotta brought most of her stuff in along with new shopping bags she quickly shoved him out the door. Not hearing the kids she went in to check on them; still fast asleep. LaRhonda heard her phone in the distance. She walked back to the living room and answered her phone. "What's up?"

"Shit . . . You spoke to Shawna lately?" Keisha lay on the bed, staring at the ceiling.

"Damn, I ain't speak to you in a minute. You got my text earlier?"

"Nah, I ain't get nothin'. I've been working a lot. So you ain't speak to Shawna? Nah she ain't tryin'a talk to my ass for nothin'." Keisha laughed nervously.

"No, you didn't!" LaRhonda laughed, bringing tears to her eyes.

"Why you laughing so damn hard?"

"'Cause, my last conversation with her she wasn't my friend and definitely not yours. How she making changes and leavin' the ghetto shit for us hood folks. Who she think she is? Oh, yeah, and how you told me you gay, but you ain't tell her." LaRhonda didn't laugh; she waited silently for Keisha's reaction. *Will she lie? I wonder. . . .*

Keisha sat up quickly. She didn't answer right away; she couldn't, she was cornered. "Umm . . ."

LaRhonda's ears perked up. *Will she finally confess?*

"I never told you this . . . or anybody 'round the way. Yes, I am gay." Keisha waited for the barrage of questions.

LaRhonda chose not to lie about her knowledge. "I know."

Keisha's eyes widened, raising her to her feet. "How the fuck did you know?"

"Really, KeKe, c'mon now . . . it's 'bout time you stop frontin'," LaRhonda spoke with ease.

Keisha didn't believe what she just heard. She never slipped when they were younger and even now she kept a tight lid on her escapades.

"First of all, you never got a man; second, you always in the fuckin' city down over there by SoHo. What, you think I'm stupid or that I wouldn't figure it out by now?" LaRhonda didn't let her in on her snooping skills or how much she really knew.

"You act like I ain't never had no dude. I guess you forgot 'bout that night in Hollis, Queens," Keisha reminded her.

"Hollis, Queens . . . I remember no such night. Anyway what's up with you? I saw your moms downtown, but she acted like she ain't hear me. I figured I'd hear why from you." LaRhonda changed the subject quickly; that night in Hollis, Queens was a hot mess she would never talk of.

"She kicked me out. I'm at that cheap motel by Gateway Mall," Keisha said with a little shame in her voice.

"Gateway? You rode your bike all the way over there?"

"It ain't that far for someone that exercises. Ha-ha . . ." Keisha said.

LaRhonda didn't bother to laugh at her stupid remark. "So what you gonna do? You ain't gonna stay there are you?" she asked.

"Umm, ain't nowhere else I could go. You tryin'a put me up? Where you at anyway?" Keisha asked curiously.

"Ahh . . . Well I ain't by my moms for sure. I'm in Marcy staying with . . . Eric." LaRhonda stayed silent after stating her whereabouts.

"Eric . . . Eric? How in the hell did you get him to do that? You know Vincent gonna find out and when he does he gonna pay someone to hurt you like he did it himself. You playing with fire, girl. Unless . . ." Keisha shook her head, pulling a cigarette from the Newport box on the nightstand.

"Well, what you want me to do? I'm tired of kicking my mother out the house every other fuckin' night. Everything I own including my fuckin' drawers I gotta keep under lock and key. And I ain't talkin' 'bout any little old lock on a door either. I'm talkin' 'bout doubling up. Two locks on the room door and combination locks on suitcases and shit. After the first week I had to buy both my kids shoes 'cause they fuckin' grandma done got into the room somehow and stole they shit. I'm tired of that. And if fuckin' Eric wanna play daddy then let him. 'Cause my real baby daddy ain't doin' shit but time right now. Fuck . . . I need him more than ever now." LaRhonda looked at the window, staring out at the sun beaming onto the playground's slide.

Keisha didn't know how to react to that statement. The only person LaRhonda had ever lived with was Vincent. All the other niggas she fucked was just that: niggas she fucked. They meant nothing; she seemed addicted to the lifestyle it bought: more popularity and more gifts. When she met Vincent it was abusive from the start. He demanded to see her, forced her to skip school and stay with him, ultimately impregnating her with Diamond in her junior year of high school. Keisha knew about the triangle affair she had going on and always thought Eric was Aaron's dad.

"So you ain't mad that I didn't tell you nothin' 'bout—"

"You lickin' pussy instead of suckin' on some dick?" LaRhonda laughed.

"Stop that shit okay. 'Cause it's my business not yours."

"You right 'bout that. Yup, all yours and nobody else's, just like mine," Ronnie said, giving her a hint to her privacy.

"Yeah, so what's the deal with Shawna?"

"She on her shit, again. Just 'cause we ain't disclose all our secrets we ain't friends. Oh yeah, I can't forget we ghetto, too, 'cause her boss say so. She on that 'high and mighty, she better than us' type bullshit. You know she used to do this in high school, too. Remember when I got prego and she was the last one I told? She didn't talk to neither one of us 'til Diamond was born. Then it was like she Aunty Shawna and shit. Crazy bitch, if you ask me. She just wanna always be down," LaRhonda added, putting in her hate.

"Nah, you know how she is. Is that what she said?"

"Umm, basically . . . Why you so worried 'bout what she think anyway? She'll be back wanting our input on something. Besides she workin' with that record label now and trust me she got no fashion sense or swag to keep her job." LaRhonda laughed.

"True that! A'ight so what you doin' with Eric? You know he gonna want a DNA test. I don't think he wants to take care of somebody else's child too," Keisha said.

"Who told you that? Did you talk to Eric?" LaRhonda questioned, showing some paranoia in her tone.

Keisha wasn't surprised that LaRhonda had some scheme in the works. "Damn, relax. Ain't nobody seen nobody. I told you I ain't been around. So what's really goin' on, Ronnie?"

"A'ight, I'ma be real. I didn't force Eric into letting us stay here; he suggested it. And yes, he said he wanted a DNA test and how he gonna set it up and pay for it. Between me and you I don't know if Vincent the father or if he is. Shit, when I got prego I just went with Vincent 'cause he was back and on top again. Eric was fun, but never had enough thug in him for me." LaRhonda finally admitted out loud some truth.

"So how you planning to dodge a DNA test?"

"I'm not. He said even if Aaron ain't his he gonna let us stay anyway 'cause he don't want us back my moms."

Keisha shook her head and sparked another cigarette. "Ronnie, do you believe him? 'Cause I sure as hell don't."

LaRhonda wanted to end the conversation; she sat in silence thinking back momentarily. *Nah, he couldn't be. It was just that one time and it was quick. Shit, I'm fucking scared.*

"Ronnie . . . LaRhonda, don't act like you ain't heard me," Keisha said.

"Well, we'll see. Anyway, panty-licker, I gotta go. I can hear Aaron waking up. I'll call you."

"I guess I can expect you to say shit like that now, but don't expect me not to punch you dead in yo' face if you take that shit too far." Keisha made it known not to play the name-calling game with her.

"Whateva . . . I'll call you." LaRhonda ended the call.

Sitting back on the sofa, LaRhonda could hear the kids rustling around in the room. "Damn, here we go. Diamond, don't jump on that bed; you are gonna end up hurting yo' brother." She headed for the kitchen, peeking into the bags on the countertop. "I wonder which one of these bags got yo' bottles, son. I know I brought a new pack."

She was happy that Keisha finally came out. It was hard for LaRhonda to combat the rumors floating around the hood for her much longer. But she couldn't worry about that anymore; she had bigger things to worry about.

8

Keisha

Damn, I gotta get some place to stay. This fuckin' shit is gettin' on my last nerve. Shit, it's like these motherfuckers don't die. After staying at the cheap hotel for a few nights, Keisha desperately wanted to leave. The roaches moving about made her skin crawl; every way she looked, every drawer she pulled open. *Shit, we had these bad boys but damn at least it was under control,* she thought, shaking out her knapsack over the tub. One, two, three flew out her bag . . . *Oh hell fuckin' no!*

Keisha shook her bag one last time and nothing came out. She took a small duffel bag out the closet, and packed the few hanging clothes and a small shopping bag filled with undergarments. She had one option and that was Nicole. The only downside foreseen was Nicole's stalker ways. Keisha could remember the first time she met Nicole; it was fun.

"I have a delivery."

"Okay, who's it from?" Nicole asked.

"Umm . . . Shore Real Estate. Are you going to let me in? I have other deliveries to make."

"Oh no, yo' ass comin' up here because I definitely want yo' name so I can let your boss know how rude you are."

The door buzzed loudly. Keisha walked up two flights of stairs and saw a young woman with pale white skin, deep-set blue eyes, brunette hair, and a skinny body type with her hand on her hip and a pen and paper in her hand. Damn, I could have sworn she was black.

In her most sincere voice Keisha said, *"I'm sorry, miss, but it's been a long day and I—"*

"Oh, why so apologetic now?"

Keisha didn't care what came out her mouth and wanted to see just how far she could push it. *"'Cause yo' ass white and I could lose my job!"* Keisha showed her pearly whites.

Nicole tried to keep a straight face, but eventually busted out in laughter.

"So if I was black it would still make it okay for you to be so fuckin' rude? Just come in," Nicole said, leaving the door open.

Keisha watched as she moved her unexpectedly full, round ass from side to side. She wasn't aware that there was a mirror exposing her facial expression.

"*You like what you see?*"

Keisha stood still and quickly turned her head. "Huh?"

"*It's okay, you can look.*" *Nicole smiled.*

"*Nah, I ain't like that.*"

"*You ain't like that? I can smell someone like you a mile away. I just don't see this look for you.*" *Nicole pointed to Keisha's fatigue pants and worn out green T-shirt.*

It was Keisha's turn to laugh. "*I only dress like this when I feel like it. Umm, anyway can you sign this 'cause I've already taken up too much of your time.*" *Keisha handed her the clipboard.*

Nicole licked her lips. "*Yeah, no problem, but I'ma still call yo' boss.*"

"*Wow and here I thought we were past that.*" *Keisha pouted as she reached for the clipboard.*

Nicole liked the challenge of turning girls out, especially when all they needed was a little push. "*Okay, I'll make a deal with you only 'cause you're so cute. Why don't you stop back when you get off of work later? Maybe I can dress you up a little, show you how much fun you can really have.*"

"*And you won't call my boss and try to get me fired?*"

"Depends on how much you let me dress you up," Nicole said, smiling.

After that day Keisha was introduced to another world, a free world, where no one hid their wants or needs. Nicole showed her different urges and allowed her to be herself without repercussions. Although, after a while, it seemed that Nicole had more in mind. A few times a week Keisha would stop by and they would flirt, play games, smoke a little until it became more of a routine.

Keisha wasn't ready to show herself to the people who mattered; it was more comfortable for her to play a role with people she didn't care about. Having fun with Nicole was just a pastime when Keisha didn't want to work or she needed a weed break. It became different when Nicole started calling every hour, trying to find out when she was coming by, or making plans like they was in a relationship. She wanted to go out more and more and started showing all types of PDA (public displays of affection) movements.

After Nicole showed that she wanted more Keisha slowed everything down; she stopped coming by and pumped the brakes on their intimate episodes. Keisha liked Nicole, but not enough to start a relationship or show her true colors. Now she was in a binding predicament;

she needed a place to stay. Nicole was the only person she could think of who would put her up with no questions asked, but could Keisha withstand the power Nicole would have over her?

Keisha grabbed her knapsack, threw it on her back, snatched the duffel bag off the bed, and walked her bike out the room. She headed down to the lobby to permanently check out. Keisha pulled out her phone and dialed Nicole. "Hey."

"Hey, stranger, what's up wit' you?" Nicole asked enthusiastically.

"Is yo' offer still good?" Keisha hoped she was making the right decision.

"Of course, when you comin'?" Nicole's voice was eager.

"I'll be there in an hour or so," Keisha said flatly.

Keisha handed her room key to the clerk at the desk and headed out the door. She threw the straps of her duffel bag over her shoulder and took hold of the handlebars of her bike and walked out into the night air. She decided to take the train instead of riding her bike all the way uptown; besides, she didn't think she had enough energy to make it there.

After finally making it to Nicole's house it was obvious to Keisha that other plans were in place.

"Hey, baby, I'm so happy you came," Nicole greeted her in a sheer white robe at the door.

Keisha wanted to ravish her on the spot, but didn't. Instead she rolled her bike past her and dropped the bags from her shoulders. "Damn, I'm beat."

Excited that Keisha was there Nicole rushed to close the door and hugged her from behind. "Mmm, I missed you."

"We ain't gonna get into that now. I'm tired as shit and all I want is a decent shower and a warm bed," Keisha said, prying Nicole's hands from around her waist.

"Okay, that's fine for now, but I ain't gonna go for that too long now that you staying with me. Anyway, look what I picked up for you the other day." Nicole headed to the hallway closet and pulled out a shopping bag. She reached into the bag and pulled out black and red spandex pants with a fitted shirt to match.

"Who's wearing that?"

"You don't like it? It's hot to death. Your body will have everybody drooling after you. I promise you that your tips will be bigger." Nicole smiled.

"I'm not wearing that and I don't get tips."

"Okay, we'll see." Nicole put everything back into the bag and tossed it to the side.

"A'ight, whateva . . . lemme go take a shower."

"You want company?" Nicole disrobed, revealing her nude body.

Keisha shook her head. *Damn, this may just be trouble.*

9

Shawna

It'd been a few weeks and not talking to either of her closest friends was killing her. Those were the only girlfriends she felt were real; many of her new associates faked the funk because they wanted something for nothing. All the women she met now didn't want to beat her ass like in high school, but sure as hell threw shade every opportunity they could. Making new friends and taking new steps was scary to Shawna and not having her girls around was even harder.

Shawna concentrated on the positive instead of dwelling on what she didn't have. Her job was secure, she had her own place, and best of all she had a phat bonus check. Moving her head to the tune of Bob Marley's hit "Could You Be Loved" she entered the building offices of Lifers Music in the best of moods. Happy her parents saw that she was becoming independent and needed to experience life with them from afar, her frame of mind was indestructible.

Since her promotion, Emma kissed her ass every chance that came her way; coffee was always promptly on her desk five minutes after walking in, she even arranged to have Shawna's new office painted and decorated. Shawna removed her headphones and with a huge smile greeted Emma, "Good morning; anything good happened over the weekend?"

"Good morning, Shawna. Actually, the painters finished your office and the furniture will be here today. So by tomorrow you can be in your own office instead of Carolyn's."

"That's great . . . Umm, you still going to help me with that, right?" Shawna smiled.

"Don't worry about that. I have it handled."

"Great." Shawna walked out the reception area and headed toward her temporary office. Easing behind the desk, she pressed the phone to speaker and dialed.

"Shore Real Estate, how can I help you?"

"Hello, can I speak to . . . Nicole Ashland, please?" Shawna asked, fiddling with a sticky note.

"Yes, this is her. How can I help you?"

"Hi, Nicole, my name is Shawna Vasquez. Shore referred me so we can set up a time to look at a few apartments. Do you think we can do something today?" Shawna hoped.

"That's right, I was expecting you to call me over the weekend," Nicole said, looking at her appointment book. "Okay, I have some time around two. Can you meet me then?"

"Two, huh?" She paused for a minute, staring out the window.

"Shawna, you still there? Is two o'clock okay? If not I can do four o'clock too."

"Sorry, Nicole, let's go with four o'clock. I should be able to leave the office by then."

"Perfect. I'll swing by and pick you up. See you then." Nicole ended the call.

With a smile on her face she logged on to her laptop and searched for Shore Real Estate. She clicked on one-bedroom apartments. They all looked too small for way too much money. *Was this a trick? Did I only get a bonus to pay him rent? He's a damn mogul!* She searched for studio apartments; there were none listed.

Like clockwork, Emma entered the office with Shawna's latte in hand.

"Thanks . . ." Shawna's somber tone didn't dismiss Emma quick enough.

"Wait, what happen to all the smiles you walked in with?" She peeked at the computer screen and saw the logo for Shore Real Estate.

"Ooh, I would love to live in any one of those apartments. Who popped yo' bubble?"

"Do you even know how much the rent is?" Shawna cut her down a little.

"Actually, I do. What are you so worried about? It's not like you gotta pay full price as advertised." Emma gave her a wink, suggesting other ways of payment.

"So you're telling me that these apartments come with a discount employee tag?" Shawna folded her arms across her chest in disbelief. "Emma, I really can't take your tricks today."

"Look I know we have this hate-like relationship, but you really need to start trusting me," Emma said, walking out the office.

Shawna didn't want to look foolish so she called Carolyn. After a long conversation she understood that Shore liked his people close along with his money. It made sense to want your employees to be happy enough that they don't have to worry about housing because their landlord was their boss too. But how much control of her money was Shawna willing to give? According to Carolyn, most employees lived in property acquired by the company; it was easier for most to have money taken out of their checks weekly. It wasn't a bad setup, but somehow she felt uneasy about the idea of it.

Happy that talking to Carolyn made her decision clearer, she pressed SPEAKER on the desk phone. "Hi, Nicole, I'm sorry, but I would like to cancel our appointment this afternoon."

"Oh okay, did you want to reschedule? I have an early appointment for tomorrow if that works better," Nicole offered.

"No, thank you, I will be searching for the apartment on my own, preferably non-Shore affiliated. Nothing personal, of course, just business. Thanks. Have a great day," Shawna said, ending the call.

There was no way she was going into this with her money being taken before she even got it. She stood up and headed to Shore's office. Making it clear from the start was her first order of business before stepping into her new position. Contracts weren't sealed and delivered yet. Taking her time to his office she reflected on the recent changes in her life. *Change one was the dead weight I was holdin' on to. Done. Change two is a work in progress. I'll find somewhere to live. Change three should of definitely been my número uno—my money. I can't let all the titles blind me.*

Shawna stood in front of Shore's office with her head strong and her eye on the prize. She took a deep breath before knocking the door.

"Come in," he answered.

"You have a minute?"

"Okay, let's hear it. I have a conference call in two from Japan." He gestured to the chair in front of his desk.

"I know you referred me to Nicole Ashland for the apartment hunt, but I want to find my own place. I appreciate the offer, but it would boost my confidence if I did it all on my own." She spun the reason to make her look good.

With his signature smile he said, "I wouldn't have it any other way. Is that all?"

"Actually no, I wanted to go over the money points of my contract."

"Well, we can do it over lunch. Get Emma to make us reservations somewhere close," he said, reaching for his ringing cell phone. "This is the conference call; can you close the door on your way out? Thanks."

She stepped out his office with relief and ease. Shawna headed toward the reception area with her swag back. As she got closer, the voices and laughter seemed familiar, but the who wasn't coming to her fast enough. When she finally reached the reception area, the who was standing before her—Keisha. Her entire demeanor changed in an instant; happy-go-lucky to raging fire horns in five seconds flat. She walked up to Emma. "Can you reserve lunch for two at one o'clock somewhere close? You can text me where." She fought the urge to curse both of them out.

"Okay, no problem. I tried to buzz you just a minute ago. You have a guest." Emma smiled with a wink.

Shawna rolled her eyes at Emma and turned toward Keisha. "Follow me." She walked out the office entrance and pressed for the elevator.

"Hello, Shawna, I thou—"

Shawna put her hand up, stopping Keisha from any further humiliation to herself; she looked like a fucking train wreck. She hurried her into the elevator and pressed the LOBBY button. The wink from Emma already told her this shit was going to get around quickly. Keisha's look alone would cause anyone to jump to conclusions.

"I'm sorry. I didn't mean to just show up here. I had a delivery 'round the corner. And you didn't return any of my calls. I just want to apologize for what I said. I'm really sorry. I was dealing with a lot."

Shawna looked up to the digital floor indicator without expressing words or emotions. The elevator doors opened.

Shawna stepped quickly off the elevator and out the building. Keisha lagged behind her, calling out her name, but she wasn't going to say one word to her until she was away from prying ears and eyes. Her business was her business.

"Shawna, what the fuck? You really not talkin' to me?" Keisha stood before her with a desperate look on her face.

"Keisha, are you gay?" Shawna asked in a low tone.

Keisha looked at her strange at first, but then came clean. "Yes. You mad?"

"Mad? Why would I be mad 'cause you gay? I'm mad 'cause you ain't tell me, but go tell Ronnie about it, c'mon. You talk about friends; you really ain't my friend." Shawna waited for her response with an angry stare.

"First, I'm sorry; and, yes, I shoulda told you long time ago. Second, I ain't never tell Ronnie nothin'. Is that what she told you?" Keisha stepped back with her arms crossed over her chest.

"You are . . ." Shawna dropped her head low and flashbacks of when they were younger moved her emotions into mortification.

Keisha watched Shawna's display of humiliation. She reached for her but Shawna jumped back. *No, this bitch didn't just look at me like that!*

"Well, you don't need to show up to my job 'cause you think you can. Let's be clear, you can't show up here unless you're invited. I'm no intern now. This is my job and future and all this drama shit I don't need. I can't be seen with . . . I just can't be involved in the shit you caught up in anymore. I ain't called you back for a reason. You and Ronnie can keep y'all bullshit to yo'self. Like I told you before y'all gonna be lookin' in while I'm the show. I got my shit together. I got my own place where I ain't surrounded by hustlers and closeted addicts. My future looks brighter now that y'all ain't feedin' stupid shit in my ear." Shawna didn't hold back.

"So what, now you think you better than us 'cause you got some little fuckin' job?" Keisha asked boldly.

"Nah, I don't think I am. I know my little job gonna get me further than what you do. Listen I gotta get back to work. You should too." Shawna turned around and headed back into the building, leaving Keisha standing by herself.

She felt good telling Keisha off, but Shawna knew that dismissing their friendship was harsh. Unfortunately, she felt it was something she had to do before it dragged her back into any unwanted mess.

When she got back into the office, Emma quickly tried to get into Shawna's business but she shut it down by walking straight past her without a word. *I can't believe she came up here without even talking to me first. I ain't feelin' that shit. What the fuck, am I suppose to act like ain't nothin' happen? After what we been through. I should've kept my mouth shut that night. I hope she don't . . .*

An unexpected knock at the door shook her out of her thoughts. "Come in . . ." She quickly shuffled some papers on the desk to look busy.

"Hey there, how's it going?" Shore asked, stepping into her office.

"Great, actually. Emma said my office should be done tomorrow. Is there something you want me to do?"

"Yes, I need a favor. Usually I would tell Emma to do these kinds of things, but I think it would be better if you handled it. I don't want any lines crossed." Shore shifted his brows.

"Sure, what do you need?" Shawna was ready for any distraction.

"There's a client I need you to have dinner with and explain our contract clauses to. You think you can handle that?"

"Sure, but don't you think our legal team could explain it better than me?" Shawna asked.

"Yes and no. I don't want to scare him with all the legal stuff right off the bat. I want you to hook him first. Think of it as your first big test. If he likes what he hears then at our meeting he'll just sign on the dotted line."

"Test?" Shawna said, confused.

"Maybe test is the wrong word. Let's just say I feel more comfortable. Nothing shady, it's just this client is young and still lives in the hood. So I think you would make him more at ease than Emma. He's young and hot with his lyrics. If we sign him we'll be in the money," Shore reassured her.

"Okay, I guess I'll arrange a car and reservations. What's his name?"

"Jeremy; he's local and underground. Not a lot of people know about him and he has a regular nine to five so he's hungry. You can get his info from Emma. Sorry, but we are gonna have to cancel lunch. I have to meet with Rich Mafia; some bullshit went down in Miami. We'll handle it first thing when I get back," he said as he was walking toward the door.

"Okay, but first thing when you get back," Shawna said, rising to her feet. She was disappointed; she needed to get her contract straight.

As Shore walked out she dialed Emma. "Can you cancel the lunch reservations and make it dinner at Blue Ribbon in Brooklyn? Also, call this Jeremy person and let him know what time the dinner will be. Have the car pick me up first and text me his info. Thanks." She hung up the phone.

She glanced at her watch: 11:50. *Well, I might as well go home since I'll be working later. I'll go get my hair and nails done. That should waste some time until my dinner date with this Jeremy. Why does that name sound so familiar to me?* Shawna grabbed her purse and headed out the door.

10

LaRhonda

Two weeks later . . .

God, please let this turn out the right way. She prayed silently before opening the envelope with the DNA results.

The probability of Mr. Eric Barnes not being the biological father of Aaron Williams is 100 percent. Therefore concludes that Mr. Eric Barnes is not the father of Aaron Williams.

"Holy shit! Then he is Vincent's," LaRhonda said with slight uncertainty in her voice.

Keisha looked at her with a smirk. "Damn, sounds like you still unsure."

"Umm, no . . . it was only outta those two," she said, diverting her eyes everywhere but Keisha's way.

LaRhonda's avoidance was definitely a sign that she was hiding something more.

Keisha pushed, "Ronnie, what's up? Do you need to test Vincent too?"

LaRhonda was embarrassed to admit she was looser than ever after Diamond. She looked at Keisha. "Don't judge me, okay?"

"Ronnie, you can't be serious right now. I'm like yo' sister."

"There was someone else," LaRhonda said reluctantly.

"Who?"

LaRhonda knew that question was coming, but she wasn't ready to reveal the entire truth. "Some random dude from Marcy I knew. It was one of those nights where everything was goody. Liqs, weed, shit I can even remember half the night."

"What you gonna tell Eric?" Keisha asked.

LaRhonda wanted to lie, but she knew Keisha could see right through her.

"You gotta tell him something even if you plannin' to lie." Keisha knew the answer already.

"He don't care."

"Umm, he cares 'cause he got you staying here. Let's say you don't tell him, then what? You still gonna be second-guessin' Aaron's daddy aren't you? Shit, I don't wanna see yo' ass on *Maury* either." Keisha laughed hard.

The front door suddenly unlocked. Quickly, LaRhonda tucked the paper and envelope under the cushion of the sofa.

"Hey, Eric," LaRhonda greeted him.

"Hey." He was surprised to see Keisha sitting on the sofa as he entered.

"Eric, you know Keisha right? She just stopped by to check on me. Umm, you hungry? I could make you somethin' real quick." LaRhonda tried to change the awkwardness in the room.

"Nah, I'm good. Where the kids at?" Eric asked.

"Aaron's asleep and Diamond watchin' TV in the other room."

Keisha sat there as Eric stared. It was obvious he needed to say something to LaRhonda alone. "A'ight, Ronnie, I'll check you later. Later, E," Keisha said, giving dap to Eric, walking toward the door.

LaRhonda felt a little uneasy with Eric's tone and was happy Keisha exited when she did. She didn't want Keisha to think she didn't have everything in check.

"Do you have anything to tell me?" Eric stared at her.

LaRhonda could tell he had something on his mind. *Could he already know?* The question entered her mind as she walked over to the sofa.

Contemplating telling the truth or lying, she watched him closely.

"Is there something wrong, LaRhonda?" Eric asked suspiciously.

Slowly she removed the paper stuffed under the cushion. *You better turn on the waterworks*, she voiced in her head. She stepped closer to him and handed over the paper.

"I don't need to see it," he said, pushing the paper away.

LaRhonda's crocodile tears began to fall. "You know? How you know?"

"Why you cryin'? Ain't nothin' for you to cry about." He looked at her face and couldn't feel any emotions; her actions were empty. "You didn't think you was the only one gettin' the test results did you? We knew there was only a possibility that I could have been the daddy. So what? He's Vin's; he'll be happy when he find out," Eric said in a flat tone.

Her fake tears turned into fear. "What you mean, he'll be happy when he find out? I ain't talk to him since our last visit and that was a couple of weeks ago. And I definitely didn't answer any calls from his ass on purpose." Her voice suddenly changed to the rough and tough chick she was known to be. "He can't just take the test like that without them notifyin' me." Her eyes widened.

"Ahh, there we go." Eric took a seat on the sofa, leaving her standing. "I mailed his ass a copy of the results and some pics of the kids. I thought that would be cool with you. You ain't tryin'a to be with him are you? "

She swore steam appeared from her ears. *How could he be so disrespectful to me?* she thought. Too many scenarios were playing in her head. LaRhonda was infuriated.

"What's the matter, Ronnie? You ain't mad are you?" he asked with a grin on his face.

LaRhonda looked at his face. She wanted to smack him. *Why the fuck is he grinnin' though?*

"A little birdie whispered in my ear 'bout some things for some time now and they had a lot of shit to say 'bout you."

A somber look came over LaRhonda's face. "Who were you talkin' to?"

"C'mon, did you think it wasn't gonna come out? Truthfully, I pretty much beat the shit outta him to get him talkin'. I just didn't think it was true."

"And who you had to beat on to get this lame-ass shit you sayin' to me?" She rolled her eyes, quickly jumping to her feet.

"Scared that shit gonna catch up to you?" He laughed, rising up from the sofa.

"You know what, Eric, what is all this shit? I actually thought you wasn't like the rest of these niggas out here. I thought you was tryin'a build somethin' with me. Nobody ain't hold no gun to yo' head, forcing me to come here, remember? You invited me," she said, trying to flip it on him.

"Build somethin'?" He had to laugh. "I can't build nothin' wit' a liar or a cheat. And sure as hell nobody I can't trust." Eric shifted a little to the left to retrieve a folded paper tucked in his back pocket. He unfolded it. There were three pages. Eric handed over the last page to LaRhonda.

Her face said it all; real tears appeared. The reality of her loose actions was before her in black and white.

"What the fuck is this?" She threw the paper at him and sobbed, holding her face. LaRhonda wanted to run like those girls do on *Maury*.

"Do you want to come at me with the truth now?" Eric watched as she held her wet face.

"Why did you do that? Vin gonna kill me when he get out," she screamed out.

"I ain't do nothin' but help yo' lyin' ass out. I actually fuckin' cared for yo' ass. I fuckin' fell for yo' dumb shit, too. But you see that's what makes me different from any one of these niggas out here. I'm willin' to do for yo' ass regardless.

You ain't wonder why I ain't fuck you yet?" He arched his brows.

She didn't answer.

"You better start sayin' somethin' 'cause I been the one playin' daddy for both 'em kids in there. Or did you forget 'bout 'em times you had to hide out with Diamond 'cause Vin was tappin' that jaw too many times."

LaRhonda's sniffles stopped instantly with his harsh reminder. She stood there, replaying every close-to-death beating she'd gotten from Vincent. *He know he wrong for doin' that shit! Now he wanna act like I ain't supposed to be mad. Shit, he better have a place for me to stay after all this shit.*

"Look I ain't no cold nigga. I had feelings for you even with all the shit you did, but that sneaky shit rubs me the wrong fuckin' way. I don't want any harm for you or 'em kids so like I told you from the start, it don't matter if I ain't Aaron's father. I'ma still look out for you," he said, hoping she would understand what he was about to say next.

LaRhonda hid her relief when those words left his mouth. Her sobbing eased a little, but the thought of what Vincent was going to say or do put fear into her. She started pacing the floor.

"Listen, I didn't wanna tell you this before, but I guess since the DNA came back it's only right I tell you. I'ma be headin' outta state in a few days to make some extra dollars. I'ma leave you some dough, but it's gonna have to hold you down 'til I get back." Eric grabbed her shoulders and looked at her. "You okay?"

LaRhonda wiped the wetness under her eyes with her fingers. "Why would you still help me out?"

"That don't matter."

LaRhonda didn't know how to feel. This was the first person doing anything close to good for her without wanting something in return. But there she was taking all he could give like every man who came into her life.

"But on some real shit, you gotta get somethin' poppin' 'cause my pockets ain't that deep for too long. So I hope you got a plan. Besides, I ain't gonna be comin' through like that no more. You got my number and if you need anythin', you call me." He squeezed her hand and kissed her on her cheek.

So you ain't really gonna help me. I shoulda figured like every man who's ever said that same shit. You ain't gonna do but so much or until you get tired of the shit, she thought, feeling more alone than the day Vincent got locked up.

"I'll talk to you later." He turned slowly toward the door.

"So that's it, Eric? You act like you here for me and act like you daddy. But yet you gonna leave when you dropped this fuckin' bomb in my lap. Why would you send him the fuckin' results? What do you think is gonna happen when he gets that shit?" LaRhonda started to pace the floor again.

All the anger seeped back in and she wanted to bash his head against the door. LaRhonda didn't want the reality of Aaron's father being a different man from Diamond's. Now her label and stereotype truly fit her: hood chick with different baby daddies with nothing good about her.

Deep down she wanted him to stay and play house until she got tired of it, but she knew that wasn't going to happen now. Since she moved in with him it'd been a solid routine giving her stability; without him there she didn't know if she could have handled it on her own. She was at a loss without knowing her next move. *Now what the fuck am I supposed to do? I thought this was gonna work for now. I don't got nobody to fall back on.*

Eric watched as her wheels turned and her pacing got quicker. "I'ma go now. I'll check on you. A'ight?"

"So what, Eric, I'm supposed to act like shit is good 'cause you lettin' me stay here? You done fucked up my whole shit. I can't believe you did that shit. Aaron was the only reason he stopped beatin' on me. Now you put all that anger and power back into his hands. This ain't gonna be good for me. You happy 'bout that?" she said, hoping to make him feel regretful.

"You ain't gonna lay that guilt trip on me right now. You better think 'bout how you gonna explain that shit to Vin." He opened the door and walked through, letting it slam and lock on its own.

This motherfucker done started a shit storm for my ass. I better try to cover my tracks. I need Shawna. He'll believe her over Keisha any day. Shit, that bitch ain't even talkin' to my ass! LaRhonda's thoughts of a quick cover-up may have been harder than she wanted. There were still a few days to construct a plan before Vincent would get those results. She continued to pace the floor, praying that USPS would somehow lose the mail.

11

Shawna

It felt so good to see the first-class attitude that came her way once she moved away from the hood. Although her new friends were those of business, it didn't affect her socially; it only enhanced it. Her apartment was on the second floor of a brownstone nestled off the path of the downtown bustle of Brooklyn. Cumberland Street was lined with trees, renovated brown-stones, and young, artistic city adults thinking that it was actually the "hood." The atmosphere oozed "young" swag and Shawna was finally in the middle of it.

It'd been awhile since Ronnie or KeKe tried to reach out to her. *If it was that easy to drop me then they wasn't my friends from the start,* she thought as she hustled to catch the elevator to the Lifers Music offices. Did she miss the drama they came with? Yes, she did, but she wouldn't dare admit to it.

Once stepping off the elevator and through the doors Emma greeted her with a mouthful. "Good morning, Shawna. No schedule changes, but Mr. Hughes insisted on waiting for you in your office. I tried to get him to make an appointment, but he said you wouldn't mind."

Shawna subdued her eagerness to rush into her office. "Umm . . . that's okay. Are there any messages for me?" Her continuous tapping of her foot gave Emma the impression of impatience, which covered her true feelings.

"No messages, Shawna, but Shore would like a brief word with you once he gets in." Emma smiled.

"Okay, can you buzz me when he comes in? Thanks." Shawna stared over Emma's head into the conference room for a moment. Briefly her movement paused as she remembered the feeling of strong arms embracing her, soft, full lips kissing above her waist just the way her—

"Shawna, Mr. Hughes is in your office; did you forget?" Emma asked.

Snapping out her little trance she turned and headed to her office, trying not to step too fast.

Jeremy Hughes stood five foot nine with a well-toned body. His dark curly hair, strong facial features, and light brown eyes made him a good looker to most women. He stood over

Shawna's desk scanning her VIP invites, scattered CDs, memo pads, different-colored sticky notes, and receipts layered from edge to edge.

Shawna got closer to her office; the door was left wide open. There he stood, tall and handsome, hovering over her desk. She walked into her office, closing the door behind her. "Hello." She smiled.

"Come here, mmmm . . . you smell so good," Jeremy said, pulling her closer and nibbling her neck.

"Stop, *papi*, not here. You know what that does. I won't be able to control myself." She giggled, moving her neck away. "Jeremy, I told you we can't act like that here. Professional, remember?"

Suddenly her door opened. She was in the arms of Jeremy with a caught look on her face. There Shore stood before them. Shawna quickly backed away from Jeremy.

"Shawna, can I speak to you in my office please?" He was still standing in the doorway.

"Shore, it's not what—"

"In my office now, Shawna!" Shore snapped as he turned toward his office.

Shawna knew her job and her budding career could be over. She looked to Jeremy. "I'm finished." She slowly headed to Shore's office.

"Close the door," Shore said, standing close to his desk. "Shawna, do you know why I hired you?"

She looked at him with tears in her eyes. "Am I fired?"

Shore laughed. "If I fired every employee who crossed the line with a client I wouldn't have a staff."

Her heartbeat slowed. She took a seat on the single chair in front of his desk. "I didn't mean for this to happen. It just did."

"So, what, you went to dinner then opened your legs?" Shore didn't hold back.

"No, it wasn't even like that. That dinner was all business and you know it 'cause the next day he signed the contract without any lawyer present, just the way you wanted. It wasn't until I bumped into him a couple of days later did it progress into something more."

"I should have realized that you would fall for a hood nigga like that. I thought you had something, but I guess I was wrong. I trusted you enough to think this type of shit wouldn't happen. I thought you were ready. Get out of my office and I don't want to see your face for a couple of days." Shore watched her jaw drop, standing behind his desk.

Shawna's tone changed from soft to harsh in an instant. "Hold up, Shore, who do you think you're talking to? I did my job and you got what you wanted. So what if I want something more with him? That's my business. Who the fuck are you? This is not what I signed up for. You can't control my personal life." She stood up, ready to walk out.

"Shawna, you don't even know shit about this nigga, but yet you spreading yo' legs. I thought if you crossed any line it would be with me," his honesty spilled.

She was shocked, then confused. There was a long pause before she finally said, "What makes you think I fucked him?"

His head dropped a little; then he stepped closer to her. "That ain't my business, but wasting your time with these young toys when you need . . . a real man in your life . . . like me."

"Are you saying that—"

Shore reached for her hand. "This is not how I imagined telling you my feelings, but honestly, when I saw you in that . . . in your office, I knew I had to tell you. Yes, I am attracted to you and yes, I do want to see if it can go further."

Shawna moved her hand slowly. Her voice was trapped in her head. *You can't be fuckin' serious. Now he wants the cookie. I can't believe this shit!* She walked out his office without a word. Passing her office on her way toward the reception area's front doors she saw Jeremy still in her office. She stopped at the door.

"Is everything okay?" Jeremy moved closer to the door.

"No, but this can't continue," Shawna said, quickly moving past him toward her desk.

"What? I thought—"

"You thought wrong. This ain't what I want or need. I'll have Carolyn call you to set up your studio time and arrange a producer for you. Now please just leave." Shawna turned her back toward him, indicating that she was not taking any pleas.

When she heard the door close she let out a sigh. She plopped into her chair and sat there, staring into the air. Her phone buzzed. UNKNOWN CALLER flashed across the top of the screen on her cell phone. She pressed END.

There was a knock at her door; then Shore entered her office. "Shawna, can we talk?"

Shawna's nerves prevented her from speaking; she just nodded.

"I don't want you to feel uncomfortable and I definitely don't want to lose you as an employee. So, how we going to fix this?" He leaned against the door.

Shawna just sat there staring at him with questions swirling about in her head. *What do I do? Should I even get involved with this man? Is this shit for real?*

"Shawna, can you say something? You're scaring me."

Clearing her throat she whispered, "Are you serious?"

He moved toward her desk. "Yes."

"This can't be happening. I thought you didn't want my panties." She forced a smile on her face.

"I didn't and I still don't, at least not yet," he joked. "I said I want to see where this can go. If I wanted a whore I would have hired one."

"Damn, you didn't have to say it like that. I don't know. This seems like it could be messy." Shawna spoke the truth. She didn't want to be known as the boss's girlfriend. "What if it doesn't work out? Then what, we go back to normal? I really doubt that."

"Why? Oh, let me guess, Emma's filled you in." He rolled his eyes and took a seat in front of her desk.

"Actually no, but you could." She waited for his response.

"She was a one-night stand before we were even Lifers Music. It meant nothing and will never be anything. She works here as a favor to my partner. Yeah, she gets into everybody's business and creates some of her own but she's manageable."

"Wait, you mean you and Emma?" Shawna laughed loudly and a sense of reprieve came over her.

"It's not that funny and something I definitely am not proud of. Now can we move forward, because I need to get back to work, but I would like to take you out tomorrow night. What do you say?"

Shawna closed her eyes. "Okay, let's see where it goes."

"Good. Just one thing: Can we keep this to ourselves for now?"

"I was thinking the same thing."

Shore took her hand and kissed it, then walked out her office with a smile on his face.

Shawna's phone started to blast salsa music, indicating it was her mother on the line, "*Hola,* Mama, what's up?"

"Umm, you coming for dinner tonight? I made your favorite."

"Yeah, I'll be there. I love you; see you later." She hung up the phone quickly, not wanting to get into a full conversation with her.

For the rest of the day there was a nervous tension between Shore and her. She kept to herself in her office and left early, avoiding Shore and everyone else. Her mind kept telling her this was something she could use to her advantage. She'd already gotten this far without any drama, but she needed to think about her next move carefully. *Damn, I wish I could bounce some shit off Keisha and LaRhonda.*

A few hours later she was back in her old hood, walking to her mother's house from the train station. Suddenly someone tugged on her bag. She spun around quickly. "Who the—"

"Hello . . ."

"What you doin' 'round here?" She was a bit scared to see Jeremy.

"You forgot I was from over here. Yo, what really happened today? I thought you was feeling me; at least, that's what you said when I was knocking your back out a week ago. What happened?" he asked loudly.

Shawna felt embarrassed by his tone. "Lower your voice, Jeremy. You almost cost me my fuckin' job."

He stepped in front of her, preventing Shawna from moving forward.

"Excuse me." Shawna tried to push through him.

"Nah, you owe me an explanation. I ain't just no regular nigga you can play like that. I have a reputation." He folded his arms across his chest.

"I don't owe you anything and I definitely don't owe you an explanation. So I suggest you keep it moving, Jeremy. I think you forget who I am and what I can do to that reputation of yours before it got put to use." She stepped back, feeling empowered.

He laughed. "Do you really think you got power over there? Shit, is that why yo' girl Emma put me on to yo' game? Look I'm in it to win it so trust me if a scandal is behind my name it'll just be a boost. You ain't nothin' in this industry unless there's some kinda scandal behind you and if the label wants it, I'm game, baby. I'll make sure to tell Shore why it was so easy to sign that contract." Before he could walk away he heard his street name being called: "Shotta."

Humiliated by his words and attitude she bowed her head and turned to walk away when she heard a familiar voice behind her.

"Shotta, where you goin'?"

Shawna turned around to see LaRhonda standing next to Jeremy. "Ronnie?" She had to look harder because it'd been awhile since she saw Ronnie last. Her hair was shorter and it seemed that she lost a lot of weight; almost too much.

"Oh shit," LaRhonda said, surprised to see her.

"Ronnie, you know her?" Jeremy asked, stunned that their worlds were closer than he thought.

"Yeah, that's my girl. You better not be tryin' nothin' with her," she joked with him, but soon discovered it was the wrong thing to say.

"Too late, I already did," Jeremy said, walking away pissed off.

"What the hell was that about?" LaRhonda asked.

Shawna wasn't laughing and wasn't about to give in to the drama. "Nothing."

"You know he just signed some record deal so now he think he hot shit."

"I know; he signed with my label." Shawna rolled her eyes.

"Look at you." LaRhonda stepped away, checking out her new Manhattan look. "I guess workin' for that label made you step up your game in the style department. I missed you." LaRhonda reached out to hug her, hoping to bury their little misunderstanding.

LaRhonda's friendly attitude threw Shawna off; she didn't return the friendly hug. Their last conversation wasn't very pleasant and she hadn't talked to her since. She wondered if her embrace was sincere or was there something up Ronnie's sleeve.

"If you missed me why you haven't called me?" Shawna asked, standing still.

"I did, you just didn't pick up. Don't front after you cussed my ass out and you put me and KeKe out to dry. I can't believe you got mad that KeKe didn't tell you she was gay. That's her business. Sorry if you didn't want to hear it the way I said it, but you act like you didn't already know." LaRhonda tilted her head a bit, letting it all out.

Shawna watched her closely; her words opened a dark box. "What do you mean by that?"

"Look I ain't tryin'a dig into anyone's closets. Can we just move pass all this shit?" LaRhonda knew bringing up her dark secret would get her back in line.

"I guess. So, you going to yo' mama house?" Shawna started to walk toward the projects.

"Nah, I ain't there no more. I'm over in Marcy now, chillin'. The kids don't gotta see the bull-shit with my mom and we got a decent place to ourselves. I don't gotta worry 'bout nobody bustin' my door in and stealin' my shit no more." LaRhonda smiled.

"Oh well, that's good. I'm headin' to my mom's for dinner. You wanna come?" Shawna invited her.

"Umm, I don't know. I gotta go get the kids from Mary then head home 'cause Eric said he was comin' through," Ronnie replied.

"Eric? You back with him now?" Shawna stopped and stared at her.

"No, I'm not, but he's helping me out for now until I can . . . well, you know, until I can get somebody to take care of me," LaRhonda admitted.

"Okay, I guess I'll see you around then," Shawna said.

"How's that when you don't even live over here no more? I heard 'bout you movin' out. You know them heifers in the building nosey as shit. There was even a rumor that yo' parents kicked you out."

"How you know I moved? When I was callin' you and Ronnie to help ain't nobody pick up their phones." Shawna sucked her teeth.

"C'mon, I was goin' through my own shit, Shawna. You livin' it up from what I hear. You got yo' own place, doin' what you want to do. Let's be for real, you don't want nothin' to do with me or KeKe anymore." LaRhonda's voice became loud.

"Why you say that? I'm busy. I guess you forgot I'm tryin' to get my name out there. Do you think I want to go back to school? How long do you actually think my parents gonna go for this? They expected me to go to college and when I convinced them this what I wanted to do my father told me if a year passes and I don't excel, I will be back at home and going to school."

"So what?" LaRhonda shrugged her shoulders.

Shawna looked at her strange. "You used to say that the hood was for losers. Now you want to be here?"

"I never said that. Don't put words in my mouth. All I'm sayin' is would it be that bad? Shit I still live in the hood, just a different hood. Ain't nothin' wrong wit' that."

"You crazy. I don't wanna be around here," Shawna responded.

"Then you rather not be 'round KeKe and me 'cause we from here. Shawna, don't forget where you came from. Don't let all that good shit get to yo' head," LaRhonda snapped at her.

"What's that supposed to mean?" Shawna questioned.

"Nothin', I'm just sayin'. I woulda told you that Shotta was a nobody and giving him the cookie would be a strike all around." LaRhonda stopped at the front of the building. "Okay, so when we all gonna get together? Besides, you gotta show KeKe and me your new place. You know you need help decorating. You probably still sleepin' on yo' air mattress." LaRhonda laughed.

It was true, she was still sleeping on her air mattress only because she couldn't decide on what kind of bedroom set to get. Shawna rolled her eyes and admitted, "Yeah, you right." Shawna would never admit that all her swag was a mixture of LaRhonda's and Keisha's inputs. They had always been there and turning her back on them now only seemed ridiculous. They were her friends; closer than anyone in her life now.

Shawna pulled her phone out and texted LaRhonda her address. "There, why don't y'all swing by sometime? I'm sure we got a lot to catch up on." Shawna smiled, hugging her.

"Okay. I'll call KeKe 'cause she probably still mad at yo' ass for talkin' the way you did to her."

"Oh, she'll live," Shawna said, waving good-bye.

Shawna didn't want to admit it, but it felt good seeing LaRhonda; it made her feel better. It was good to see a real face instead of the fake ones she saw on most days. She walked into the building and headed to her parents' apartment. Shawna thought about what LaRhonda said about her still sleeping on her air mattress. *Who does she think she is? At least I got my own place. What does she have?*

12

Keisha

The lights were extremely dim and music
was playing softly when Keisha entered Nicole's
apartment. *Oh c'mon, I ain't with this shit.* She
was beginning to think living with Nicole was
a huge mistake. Keisha wasn't prepared to have
a relationship. Outing herself to her friends
was easy, but outing herself to the world was a
different story.

Since Nicole allowed Keisha to stay with
her there was an underlining eeriness to her.
After the first night Keisha caught her snooping
through her duffel bag. She covered up the
snooping pretty well by convincing Keisha that
she was only putting her stuff into a drawer she
cleared out for her. Then Nicole presented her
with a key immediately, which was super weird
to Keisha because they had only been intimate a
few times since they met. Later that same week

Keisha caught her again when she came out the shower. Nicole was fiddling with her phone. When Keisha snatched it away and looked at her phone the picture of Shawna and her was on the screen letting Nicole know that she had competition.

The first week was what Keisha thought to be just Nicole being nosey because she caught some feelings. But when the questions became frequent and the repeated text messages entered a new realm of annoyance, Keisha tried keeping her distance by working constantly and staying away from the apartment as much as she could. But when Nicole started arguing about money and Keisha didn't have it, showing love was the easiest thing to do behind closed doors.

"Nicole . . ." Keisha yelled, propping her bike against the wall of the hallway.

Suddenly a shadow passed through the kitchen toward Keisha. "Hello, baby. I'm glad you're home," Nicole whispered and walked closer.

With the dim light hitting Nicole it seemed as if she was nude in red six-inch Jimmy Choos. At a closer look she was sporting a nude-colored mesh crotch-less body suit. "What's this about?" Keisha asked, walking pass her toward the kitchen, heading to snatch a drink out the fridge.

"I thought we'd make it official tonight and stop pretending to just be roommates. I care for you. I wonder where you are, who you with, when you coming home because, I'm cooking dinner for you. Keisha, there's nothing I won't do for you," Nicole said from across the room.

When Keisha heard Nicole's words she choked on the OJ entering her mouth. She had a strange feeling that this was going to happen. Keisha didn't have a clue on what to say. Staying with Nicole was out of desperation and now it was obvious she expected more.

"Keisha, talk to me. I just spilled my heart out and you have nothing to say? This is what I'm talkin' about. If our communication ain't right, I won't know what's going on with you. Now talk to me," Nicole insisted with her arms folded across her chest.

Keisha felt trapped. There was nowhere to run. With juice spilling from the sides of her mouth she answered, "I don't wanna sound ungrateful, but I don't want this. I don't want to be in a relationship. I don't want the constant contact. I need some space." Keisha flicked on the kitchen light switch to see Nicole's reaction.

"Space? You have your space. I'm not on top of you twenty-four-seven. If you felt that way about it why continue to sleep in my bed then?"

Nicole walked over to the stereo and pushed the off button.

"You invite me into your bed every night since I came up in here. I'll sleep on the sofa if that's what it'll take for you to slow yo' ro'. Look, I do appreciate everything you doin' for me right now, but if this what you want I can't continue to stay here. That's on some real shit," Keisha said, walking closer to her.

"Oh I get it. So when you was fucking me that meant what exactly? Was it just 'cause I let you stay with me?"

"Come on, now; you and I both know what that was. Strictly sex, nothing more," Keisha answered, hoping to shut her down a bit.

"Really, just sex, right. So who was that on your phone? Is that who you want to be with?"

Keisha looked at her funny. "What are you talkin' 'bout now?" Keisha looked confused, not knowing who she was talking about.

"Give me yo' phone and I'll show you." Nicole put her hand out.

"Why should I give you my phone? So you can break my shit? C'mon, ma, I ain't that stupid." Keisha had to laugh at her request.

Nicole rolled her eyes and walked over to the dining table, picking up her cell phone. She turned to Keisha and handed it to her. "Here, take my phone. If I break yours you can break mine; that way we in the same boat."

"Like you don't have two more just like it," Keisha said, reaching into her back pocket, taking out her phone. "I swear, Nicole, if you break my shit I'm smashing yo' phone and everything in this bitch."

Nicole rolled her eyes and snatched the phone out Keisha's hand. Quickly she pressed on the screen, and then she faced the phone for Keisha to see.

On the screen showed the one picture of Shawna naked on LaRhonda's bed. Keisha took that picture the night Shawna was drunk and allowed her kissing to go further.

"That's my best friend. I took that pic so she could send it to her boyfriend. I just never erased it out my phone," Keisha lied.

Nicole looked at Keisha with a smirk on her face. "Is that why you got that only pic in a so-called hidden folder on your phone?"

She was caught. The pic was loaded into a hidden folder. The only question in Keisha's mind was, how in the hell did she figure out her password? Keisha took her phone out Nicole's hand. "How did you get into that?" Keisha's asked seriously.

"You don't worry about that. Just tell me the truth."

"It is the truth!" Keisha screamed.

"You know what, Keisha, I think you right. This ain't gonna work out; maybe you should just leave." Nicole's voice trembled with tears falling from her eyes.

"It's midnight right now; where the fuck you want me to go?"

"Why don't you go back to that roach motel you was staying at. But before you leave you owe me at least a G for putting you up for these past weeks." Nicole slipped out of her six-inch heels and patiently waited for Keisha to respond.

"You know what, Nicole, why is it every time we get into it and shit ain't goin' yo' way you ask me for fuckin' money? That shit is lame as hell. You know I don't got the money or else I wouldn't be staying with you." Keisha's temper was building.

Nicole could tell Keisha was upset, but her next words were proven to show Keisha's true colors. "Is it that you still don't want nobody to know you gay? You can't handle someone looking at you sideways 'cause you like pussy instead of dick? Or is it that being with me will force your ass to fully come out? You scared?"

Keisha smacked her across the face.

Nicole exited the room, sobbing, and slammed the bathroom door.

Keisha stood there momentarily, listening to Nicole cry loudly. Her whiny moans seemed to get louder. Keisha walked toward the bathroom, standing in front of the door. "Nicole, open the door," she said in a soothing voice.

The doorknob slowly turned and the door was left slightly ajar. Nicole was still sobbing.

"I'm sorry. I didn't mean to hit you. I should have never let that go down. If you want me out now I wouldn't blame you," Keisha said, standing by the door.

"I don't want you to leave. I was wrong. I shouldn't have said that. It's my fault," Nicole said, through sniffles and wiping her eyes with toilet paper tissue.

Keisha was baffled at her reaction. Anyone else would have hit the roof and tossed her out. She heard Nicole blowing her nose and washing her face. Suddenly it became apparent that Nicole had some kind of chemical imbalance.

"Let's go out. I got invites to a private party and I think it's what we both need to relieve all this tension we got." Nicole walked past her.

This girl is fuckin' nuts!

***

Two hours later Keisha escorted Nicole into the Trump Plaza hotel in SoHo. Keisha had delivered to Trump Plaza on the East Side before, but this hotel was mind blowing. At first Keisha didn't know if she even dressed correctly. Everything looked so sophisticated and perfectly in place for the convenience of any guest. As you entered you're greeted by the doorman, who showed you to the front desk. Keisha looked through the wall of glass, observing the limos pulling up in front as Nicole presented her invite to the clerk. There was even a library beyond the lobby, displaying art and thick books. Keisha could see guests sitting in awe over the pictures in one of the books on the coffee table. There was even bottle service offered while guests sat and conversed. *Damn, this gotta cost some serious bread,* she thought as the clerk handed back the invite and called someone to alert them that we were coming up.

"Nicole, I don't know about this. This is definitely out my lane. What kinda party is this?" Keisha asked in a whispered tone.

"Keisha, relax. Trust me, there will be no one here you know. I don't even know anyone here. One of my clients gave me the invite. I wasn't going to come, but she told me I would love it." Nicole hid the fact that it was a private swingers' party she was a member of.

They entered they elevator and pressed the button for the penthouse. Nicole wore a black strapless, short dress number and those same red six-inch Jimmy Choos. Her white skin made those heels the first thing you noticed on her. The elevator finally chimed and the doors opened. Nicole looked up to see which way the room was.

"4405 . . . It's this way."

As they got closer Keisha said, "I don't hear no music."

"You won't; the room is soundproof so no loud parties disturb other guests. Some people stay here for weeks. This place is crawling with old and new money from all walks of life."

"You sound like you come here a lot." Keisha got suspicious.

Nicole giggled as they rounded the corner. To Keisha's surprise there were two big, muscled-looking dudes posted outside the door. Nicole handed one of them the invite.

Keisha knew this was something serious when he pulled out a scanner and waved it over the invite. *Whose party is this?* Keisha wondered, standing there.

"Can I have your phones please?" the muscle man asked.

"My phone?" Keisha looked at Nicole.

"Just give him your phone; you'll get it back," Nicole answered.

The muscle man punched in some numbers on the pad below the doorknob and the door opened.

The music was loud and the suite was dark as they entered. They slowly walked down the hallway and that's when Keisha saw it: people everywhere in groups, coupled up or by themselves, watching. There were lit candles placed perfectly so areas were somewhat dark enough that you couldn't see from afar what exactly was going on. She stared out at the city lights through the floor-to-ceiling windows. Keisha wanted to be mad, but couldn't be. She understood why Nicole brought her to a party like this. Keisha had to see that there were people just like her hiding their truths also. There were about sixty people throughout the penthouse from what Keisha could see. She dared not move until Nicole guided her to an open area where people were talking and drinking.

"Come on, follow me," Nicole said with a huge smile.

Keisha kept looking around, scared that she might make the wrong move. Suddenly a young, super skinny black guy appeared out of nowhere, naked, with only a Knicks fitted cap and old-school Ewing sneakers on, swinging his rock-hard dick to the beat of Kendrick Lamar's latest "Bitch, Don't Kill My Vibe" remix.

"Let me get us some drinks," Nicole said.

The more Keisha looked around she noticed everyone there couldn't be any older than twenty-five. She heard about parties like this, but had never seen one up close and personal. There were hood parties that went down like this, but never this open. She thought it was funny that young people with money showed and proved there were no boundaries with anything.

Nicole returned with a bottle of Patrón and two glasses.

"How the hell you got a bottle up in here?" Keisha arched her brows, taking one of the glasses.

"So what you think?"

Keisha took the bottle and lifted the cork. Filling half her glass with the liquid she then swallowed every drop in one gulp.

"Slow down, baby. You don't have to worry about getting called out here. Everyone knows it's like Vegas—what happens in Trump stays at Trump." Nicole laughed, tickled pink with herself.

Keisha's face changed. "So you do know these parties?"

Nicole was caught. "Yeah, I do. If I told you what kind of party it was you wouldn't have come."

"You damn right, this shit is wild." Keisha poured herself another drink.

"Give me that bottle, before you get wild!" Nicole took the bottle and placed it on the table in front of her. She scanned the room and saw a familiar face. "Oh, shit!" she busted out, almost knocking the bottle over.

"What?" Keisha looked around frantically.

"We gotta go leave now."

"Hold up, you brought me here to show me a good time and now you want to leave? What kinda games are you playing, Nicole?" Keisha showed her disappointment.

Nicole got closer to Keisha and pointed at a man getting his freak on with a well-known partygoer. The only mishap was this guest had something extra than any other female of the party. Quickly Nicole got Keisha to her feet and they headed toward the suite's entrance door. She collected their phones and they swiftly went toward the elevator.

Nicole was silent in the elevator. Keisha could see that there was something messing with her mind.

As they exited the hotel Keisha stopped and turned to Nicole. "What the hell was that about? You want me to feel comfortable with everything; then you just want to leave 'cause you seen some dude fucking a tranny."

Nicole took a deep breath. "That's not it. It's who I saw."

"And?" Keisha wasn't moving until she got a full explanation for leaving.

"He's my fuckin' boss! Do you think I want him to know I get down like that?"

"You're a fuckin' hypocrite! I thought you said what happens in Trump stays at Trump. So fuckin' what he's your boss? Why does that even matter?" Keisha's voice was loud.

"Keisha, do you even know who I work for?" Nicole tilted her head and looked at Keisha with a dumb expression.

"I don't know and don't care. That's why I never asked," Keisha replied shortly.

"He's the owner of Lifers Music and Shore Real Estate."

Keisha stepped back, falling over with laughter.

"Why are you laughing? That shit ain't funny. If anybody finds out . . . Let's just say that tidbit of information can provide somebody a small house."

"What you mean?" Keisha played dumb.

"Put it this way: If you put it out there in the industry right now and hint at what you just saw, trust there would be a whole lot of magazines and music reporters knocking on your door to pay for your story. You would probably get a bigger deal if you had a picture. That's why they take your phones at the door." Nicole started walking down Spring Street away from the hotel.

Keisha wasn't following her.

"Keisha, come on; we can catch a cab back to the house," Nicole said after noticing she wasn't walking with her.

"I'm good. I'ma head to BK. I'll see you in the morning."

"You can't get back in without the invite," Nicole added.

"Please, I ain't even gonna try to go back in there. Lawd knows who else in there gettin' they assholes blown out!"

Nicole rolled her eyes and waved her hand in the air to signal a cab. Keisha waved her good-bye with a smile.

Ain't this some shit! Keisha didn't know what else to do but laugh as she walked toward the Broadway-Lafayette train station. All she knew was she had a story to tell.

13

LaRhonda

The probability of Mr. Jeremy Hughes being the biological father of Aaron Williams is 99.9 percent. Therefore concludes that Mr. Jeremy Hughes is the father of Aaron Williams.

LaRhonda remembered reading those words on the paper Eric gave to her. She'd been avoiding Vincent's calls for days. It didn't help that Diamond was bugging the shit out of her to speak to him. LaRhonda had to carry her phone around with her just so she wouldn't pick up the phone when his name showed on the screen. LaRhonda saved the number to her phone when he called so she wouldn't think it was a creditor or telemarketer.

Guilt was killing LaRhonda slowly but surely. It kept her up at night and edgy during the day. She would stare at Aaron, trying to figure out whose features he resembled. *Could I lie and get away with it?*

Her back pocket vibrated. She pulled out her phone and saw Vincent's name. Saying a quick prayer before answering she accepted the collect call.

"Oh, so you finally taking my calls now. What the fuck is the problem? Where you been?" Vincent asked.

"Trying to get a job, nigga. Remember you ain't around to take care of us anymore," LaRhonda said, lying through her teeth. She wanted him to feel like shit.

"True, true. Let me talk to Diamond for a minute," he said.

LaRhonda called Diamond out the room and put her phone on speaker. "Diamond, come talk to yo' daddy; hurry up."

Diamond came rushing out the room with a big smile. She took the phone and walked over to the sofa.

"Where you think you goin'? That ain't yours. Talk to him right here," LaRhonda said, stopping her from moving.

Diamond wasn't a stupid kid. She knew exactly what her mother was doing. She loved her father too much for him not to know the truth about where they were at. Diamond picked her words carefully as she talked to her father in front of LaRhonda. Her mother stayed close so only the "I love you's" and "miss you's" were heard. But before she handed the phone back Diamond mentioned that her favorite kids restaurant was nearby: Chuck E. Cheese's. When she said it her father reacted instantly.

"Chuck E. Cheese's, huh? Okay, baby, I love you and miss you. I'll talk to you soon. Where yo' mama at?"

LaRhonda knew that tone. He was ready to interrogate. She shooed Diamond away and took the phone off speaker. "Yeah?"

"Where you stayin' at? 'Cause I know Chuck E. Cheese's ain't nowhere near yo' mama house unless you got a car now."

"I had to move, Vin. You already know what goes on at my mother's house. Shit, you don't even know how many times I had to go buy formula 'cause her ass or whoever she had over was stealin' my shit. How long did you think that money was gonna last?" LaRhonda was happy to be talking about anything else but that piece of paper he got. She knew he got it because he talked to Diamond and didn't want to talk to Aaron. He would usually talk to him over the phone even though Aaron couldn't talk back.

"You didn't answer my question. Where the fuck you at? Or maybe I should ask who you stayin' wit'?" Vincent's voice became irritable.

"I'm stayin' in Marcy and I ain't stayin' wit' no one." LaRhonda tried to keep the conversation calm.

"How the fuck you get a place in Marcy? You got no family there. You only know niggas from over there. Now, I'ma ask you again . . . Who the fuck you stayin' wit'?" Vincent took a deep breath, knowing that soon it was going to go bad.

"Vin, what the fuck you talkin' 'bout, man? I already told you I ain't stayin' wit' nobody. Shit, just leave it alone. Just know that your kids got a roof over their heads, which you can't provide," LaRhonda got snappy with him.

"Look, bitch—"

"Who the fuck you think you callin' a bitch?" LaRhonda shouted.

"You, bitch! I only got one kid and you already know you can drop her at my mother's."

LaRhonda stayed silent. *Here it comes . . .*

"You fuckin' bitch! I can't believe I actually believed you wasn't fuckin' with dat fool! I wouldn't be in this bitch if I knew Aaron wasn't mine. I would have just taken my fuckin' child and bounced long time ago. I swear to God I would have done that shit, Ronnie. You ain't shit! You was gonna keep this shit up and make me fuckin' think Eric was the only nigga you was fuckin'. Who the fuck is Jeremy, bitch?" His temper flared almost to the point of tears in his eyes.

She continued to be silent.

Angered more by her silence he unleashed, "You nasty-ass bitch. I'm ashamed that I had a baby with yo' ass. I shoulda known you just like 'em other wretched bitches. You ain't fuckin' shit, Ronnie."

She heard his hand hit the wall. From the sound it seemed that he may have hurt himself.

"Fuckin' bitch!" he screamed loudly. "Ronnie—"

Words couldn't form and leave her mouth fast enough before he started again.

"A'ight, you ain't talkin' . . ." His tone changed drastically; he even laughed a little.

LaRhonda shook her head in disbelief of how quickly his feelings changed. Just a second ago he was calling her all types of bitch. She kept her mouth shut, not wanting to give him any more ammunition.

"A'ight, let me get comfortable . . . Oh, Ronnie, you can't actually think I was just gonna sit back and let this play out how you want it. Oh, hell no. You see what you don't know is after Aaron was born I stepped to Eric like a man and told him we needed to take a test. He agreed, but then I got locked. I got the word out that I wanted to talk to him and we did. Man, oh man, you played me like a motherfuckin' fiddle. But what he said made sense. There was no reason for me and him to want to kill each other. It was you who deceived the both of us. I know where you at in Marcy. You stayin' at Eric's mama's house."

LaRhonda's jaw dropped. *What the fuck is happenin' right now?* She continued her silence, plopping down on the sofa.

"Cat still got yo' tongue? That's okay, I got phone time. A'ight, so now you wonderin' how'd we figure out Jeremy should be tested. Well, let's just say your birthmark is in a spot that gets people talkin' about a lot of things. It just so happened that Eric said something out loud when Jeremy's demo was playing in the background. I picked up on it when I heard, 'she taste so sweet, her mama stamped her wit' a strawberry on her pink peak.' You the only female I have fucked wit' who got that kinda birthmark on the inside of they shit. Eric felt the same way I did: ain't nobody gonna know that unless they fuckin' you. You wanna start talkin' yet?" Vincent waited for a response.

She bowed her head and whispered into the phone, "It was a one-night stand, nothing more.

It was a mistake. Eric was drunk that night and passed out. I started to drink more; then Shotta walked in with some weed and more liqs. I was so drunk, I can't even tell you how we ended up in the bathroom fuckin'. I didn't think that he could be the father 'cause I only fucked him once." Her tears dried up at this point.

"Is that right?"

"I swear I didn't even think of him in this equation. He was nothin'. He ain't even here no more. Eric showed me the DNA papers. I didn't want to believe it. After he showed me I haven't seen him. He said he was gonna still help me, but I ain't call him to ask for nothin'. Vin, I'm sorry. I'm really, really sorry. Please forgive me," she pleaded.

"Forgive you? Right now I don't give two shits 'bout yo' ass! I want my fuckin' daughter at my mother's house by tomorrow and forget about her. I swear, Ronnie, if she ain't there I'ma make sure I get somebody to find you and kick yo' ass every time you leave Marcy," he demanded.

"What the fuck are you sayin'? You think I'ma just drop her off just like that and have nothin' to do wit' with my own daughter? What kinda fuckin' shit they got you smokin' in that bitch? Yo' mama ain't gonna go for that." She tried to remind him that his mother never liked her or his daughter when they stayed over there.

"Trust me, my mother will welcome her grand-daughter as long as yo' ass don't have nothin' to do wit' her." Vincent's anger reappeared.

"Whateva, Vincent . . . I ain't payin' yo' ass no mind 'cause you, my friend, can't do shit. You must've forgotten you live in a six-by-eight iron cage. You gots no rights right now." LaRhonda swallowed her fear and continued, "Trust me, ain't no fuckin' judge givin' you my child. Nigga, you got five years, and shit if you really want me to go there I will."

"Bitch, don't threaten me. You right, Ronnie, I can't do shit, but my fuckin' lawyer sure as hell can. What you think 'bout that?"

"Well, I hope he can beat 'em charges I'ma put on yo' ass. Domestic violence charges is a bitch especially when proof is showed. So why don't you come at me from a different angle. You want me to drop her off at yo' mama's for a few days or for the weekend I'm cool wit' that. But don't think I'ma just give you our daughter. You must be out yo' fuckin' mind," LaRhonda said with no apprehension of what he would do to her.

"Charges? Bitch, you got no proof. No pictures, hospital stays, or witnesses, just yo' word against mine. With your type of friends and family it'll be easy for my mother to get custody. So if *you* want to go there we can. Now drop my daughter off at my mama's tomorrow and then we can talk about your role in her life."

There was a click heard.

"No, this nigga did not just hang up the phone on me. If he think I just giving up my kid he betta have a good-ass lawyer," she said, wanting to throw her phone clear across the room.

She sat there with her mind spinning a mile a minute. *If I charge his ass it could tie him up for another two, three years at most. Can I get enough money up to bounce to the south and start a life there? Damn, I could use some weed right now.*

The knock on the door made her jump up a bit. She wasn't expecting anyone. She looked through the peephole. LaRhonda was happy to see a familiar face; she opened the door. "What the fuck you doin' here?"

Keisha entered with a partially smoked blunt in her hand and a great big smile on her face. "Wanna smoke?"

"Hell fuckin' yeah." She quickly left Keisha to get her flip-flops.

Keisha stayed by the door and sparked up in the hallway.

After a few minutes LaRhonda returned. "You won't believe the type of drama I just went through. This came right on time."

"Man, I just found out some shit that may get my pockets a little fat. But it's on some real bitch-ass shit. I gotta make a smart move." Keisha passed LaRhonda the blunt.

After another blunt and conversation about each other's dilemmas they both came to the same conclusion: they both needed Shawna to complete their plans.

14

Shawna, LaRhonda, and Keisha

Two days later . . .

It was ten o'clock on a Saturday morning and
Shawna was just opening her eyes; then she
heard the doorbell ring. "Who the fuck is that?"
She wiped the sleep out her eyes and threw the
covers back. The doorbell rang again. "Jesus
fuckin' Christ, people like to sleep late on a
Saturday!" she hollered, then went downstairs
to open the door. Through the glass in the door
Shawna was surprised to see two faces staring
back at her. She unlocked the door and opened
it.

"What's up? I figured your ass would still be
'sleep," LaRhonda greeted her.

Shawna stood there, shaking her head and
holding the door.

"Can we come in?" Keisha asked.

Shawna moved to the side and let them by. "Straight up the steps and to the left."

LaRhonda and Keisha followed Shawna's instructions and when they entered the apartment they weren't expecting what they saw.

"Wow, Shawna, this is nice," LaRhonda said, entering the apartment.

"Thanks," Shawna said, smiling.

"Damn, girl, go wash your face and brush your teeth 'cause we all gotta talk," Keisha said.

"Umm, if someone would have called my ass maybe I would have been up. Besides it's rude to show up at somebody's house with empty hands." Shawna turned her back and walked toward the bathroom.

"Oh please," LaRhonda said.

Keisha laughed and opened the fridge. "You know she right."

Shawna entered the room and took a seat on the stool by the small kitchen island. "So why y'all over here?"

LaRhonda and Keisha looked at each other then looked at Shawna.

"Don't look at me like that. The least y'all coulda did was bring me breakfast," Shawna said, rolling her eyes.

"Well if you had some eggs or something I woulda made ya yo' favorite, cheese omelet." Keisha smiled.

Shawna laughed. "Even if I did, you still wouldn't be able to cook it. I ain't got no pots!"

They all laughed hysterically.

"How you ain't got no pots? You been living here for a minute now. You got all this and you ain't even got the essentials," LaRhonda said.

Shawna rolled her eyes. She only hoped this wasn't one of those conversations that turned sour.

Keisha could see Shawna wasn't too pleased by LaRhonda's words. "Ronnie, are you gonna tell her or what? We didn't come over here and wake her up for no reason."

Shawna looked confused. "What y'all talkin' 'bout?"

"Why don't you go first, KeKe." LaRhonda took a seat next to Shawna.

"Oh my God, what the fuck is wrong with y'all?" Shawna stood up and walked over to the sofa and clicked on the TV.

Keisha walked over to the sofa and sat opposite side of Shawna.

Shawna sat there, quiet, scanning through the channels.

"Your boss is gay," Keisha blurted out.

Shawna turned her head toward Keisha. "You can't be serious. You don't even know my boss."

"Calm down, Shawna," LaRhonda commented.

"If y'all came over her to start some shit I think y'all should leave." Shawna stood up and pointed to the door.

"Damn," LaRhonda and Keisha said in unison.

"Y'all always do that shit. Y'all always want to spoil some shit when things are good." Shawna's voice started to rise.

Keisha shook her head. "First of all we came over here to see you, not to spoil nothin'. But I think you should know yo' boss is a fuckin' faggot."

"My boss is not gay, Keisha. He actually wants to be with me. I'm supposed to go out with him tonight." Shawna folded her arms across her chest with a little smirk on her face.

"Really, well what if I told you I saw him at some party gettin' fucked by a chick with a dick." Keisha started to laugh.

"That nigga don't want you, he wants the fantasy of you. If you strapped up you may just get some." LaRhonda added her two cents.

"Shut the hell up, both of y'all. What party was this? Did you see it for yourself or are you getting yo' info from another?" Shawna asked, taking a seat back onto the sofa.

"Why don't you start from the beginning wit' the story," LaRhonda said, grabbing the remote next to Shawna.

"Fine, I'll give you the short version. I met this girl name Nicole; she lives in Harlem. I used to go to her house when I wanted to slack off from work. When my mother kicked me out and I had nowhere else to go, she let me stay with her. A couple of nights ago she took me to this exclusive party at the Trump Hotel in SoHo. I didn't know what type of party until I got there. It was on some real secretive shit. They scanned the invite, had bodyguards at the entrance, and even took our phones away. The room was hot to death. Penthouse big, candles all over the fuckin' place, people naked, not naked, people watchin' other people fuck. That shit was crazy. The fuckin' windows were so big I thought I was outside on the roof."

"I didn't know yo' moms kicked you out. Why didn't you say somethin' when you came to my job that day?"

"Shawna, can you let her finish before you start yo' trip down guilt alley?" LaRhonda interrupted.

"Ronnie, shut up. Shawna, I didn't say nothin' 'cause you didn't give me enough time to tell yo' ass what was goin' on and why I came up to yo' job. Look anyway, Nicole got all crazy and shit when she peeped yo' boss, Shore. That is his name right?" Keisha asked.

"Yes. How does this Nicole know Shore?"

"She works for Shore Real Estate," Keisha replied.

Shawna arched her brow. "Hold on, you said she works for Shore Real Estate. I talked to her before. She was supposed to find me an apartment, but I told her no, I'll find one myself."

"Really, small world, huh?" LaRhonda added.

"Anyway we was at the party, just copped a bottle of Patrón; then she saw him and wanted to leave. She said she didn't want her boss to know she got down like that. So we left. I was pissed 'cause I was there and didn't get to do shit!"

"I don't believe you," Shawna admitted.

"What?" Keisha looked at Shawna with confusion.

"You must like him, don't you?" LaRhonda asked.

"What? I don't like him!" Shawna maintained.

"Oh, that's right, you like Shotta," LaRhonda said, wanting to stir Shawna up.

"Look, Shawna, all I'm tellin' you is he a frontin'-ass nigga if he tryin'a get wit' you," Keisha cut in.

"Well, let me tell you another little story. Shotta, his real name is Jeremy Hughes right?" LaRhonda asked Shawna.

"Yeah," Shawna answered.

"He's Aaron's father." LaRhonda dropped her bomb.

Shawna's eyes widened. "What the fuck is this? Y'all wanna come up in my place and ambush me with bullshit. Y'all just fuckin' jealous I got my shit together, and you want me to be in some craziness. I really think y'all should leave 'cause I don't believe either of you!" Shawna walked over to the door and opened it.

"Do you hear this chick, Keke? I guess she want proof; well I got that shit. Hand me my bag over there please." LaRhonda motioned to Keisha. She reached into her bag and pulled out a folded white paper. "Here, come read this. Then if you still don't believe me I'm done wit' you. Nobody don't care 'bout what you got, Shawna. If I wanted to bust yo' bubble I woulda never said nothin'. Shit, it woulda been a bigger laugh on you if you actually got wit' the nigga." LaRhonda unfolded the paper, set it on the coffee table, and smoothed it out with her hand.

At first Shawna thought it was a joke. *Damn, they went really far to prove this shit. Who the fuck they done got to type up some paternity results? I ain't stupid.* With doubts in her mind she walked over to the table and picked up the paper. After reading every single little line, she turned the paper over, making sure that it wasn't something just anybody could type up.

"You still don't believe me?" LaRhonda asked, standing.

"How I know you ain't just get somebody to do this for you?"

"Shawna, you so into yo'self and whateva you got goin' on that you think somebody really tryin'a get yo' shit. You can't be serious. Ask yo'self do you actually think I would want him to be my baby father? Shit, Eric left. Vincent mad as shit and threatening my ass. So do you really think I want all that shit!"

"You know what, Ronnie, let's just go. It's obvious somebody forgot who they friends are," Keisha finally said.

Shawna was embarrassed. She made a fool of herself. Why wouldn't they tell her the truth? She stopped them before they could get to the door. "I'm sorry. Please—"

"Oh please my ass, Shawna. I can't believe you wouldn't believe me of all people. Damn, it really shows that you don't even care 'bout me. Like what the fuck?" LaRhonda shrugged her shoulders and walked through the door with Keisha following.

Shawna was left standing there, replaying what just went down. She lost her childhood friends forever.

There was a knock at the door.

"I just want the paper I left," LaRhonda's voiced behind the door.

Shawna quickly picked up the paper and rushed to the door. She opened the door with a smile. "Ronnie, please stay. I don't want to lose the only true friends I have. If you and KeKe come back in here I can tell you what we can do together so we all come out on top."

LaRhonda know that Shawna could help her, only because she was smarter than any of them. LaRhonda looked to the side of her and nodded her head. Keisha appeared in the doorway, smiling.

A few hours later they were talking and laughing as they did a year ago over dominoes and grape soda.

Shawna listened to details from both of them and hatched a plan. But her first order of business was to sneak into the office and add a clause to her already-signed contract with Shore. Changing her six-month severance clause to one year would be easy. She knew exactly how to do it with no one even knowing about it. All she needed was Emma's computer. For now she would play along with his game of courting her, and reel in every dime he had to woo her over. With enough experience under her belt she knew other labels would come knocking.

LaRhonda, on the other hand, would have to deal with two different courtrooms and two baby daddies. Shawna kept her word and helped her out with the lawyer fees. With her friends at her side she went down to the police station and pressed charges on Vincent. The district attorney formally indicted him on battery and domestic violence charges. He or his mother never filed for custody for Diamond.

After she dealt with Vincent she moved on to Jeremy, otherwise known as "Shotta." By the time LaRhonda took him to court he was well known in the rap game and his pockets were deep. The back child support payment got her out the projects permanently. She was finally able to get her GED and enroll into college.

Ultimately, Keisha became more and more comfortable with her lifestyle. She was going out with females and showing the world she wasn't afraid of who she was. Keisha quit her job and stayed with LaRhonda since she needed help with the kids while she went to school. Since she was in the house so much she started a blog that led to enormous opportunities when she dropped the biggest scandal in the music industry. Spilling every detail and adding some extra mess to her blog about Lifers Music caused her computer to crash with the sudden abundance of readers.

Through it all their friendship to each other continued no matter how many fires they had to put out. It only mattered that they put them out together.

ORDER FORM
URBAN BOOKS, LLC
97 N. 18th Street
Wyandanch, NY 11798

Name (please print):_____

Address:_____

City/State:_____

Zip:_____

QTY	TITLES	PRICE

Shipping and handling-add $3.50 for 1st book, then $1.75 for each additional book.
Please send a check payable to:
Urban Books, LLC
Please allow 4-6 weeks for delivery